BLACKBIRD

The Children Of Corvus
Book One

By:

L.E. Harrison

*Previously published as: The Druids Of Blackwater Valley: Book One: Blackbird

CONTENTS

PROLOGUE
Those Who Wait

J. Lance Sr.
Ashland, Maine

"I don't like Uncle Andrew, Daddy," Jon-Jon complained. "He's mean. When's Uncle Michael coming back?"

"Shut up, stupid," hissed Sarina, jabbing a pointy elbow in her twin brother's ribs. "You're going to make Daddy upset, then he'll go away again."

"I miss Momma," he whispered, a telltale wobble in his voice. "But she's not coming back, either."

"Come here," Jonathan said, gently patting the mattress beside him. Five year-old Jon-Jon scrambled onto the bed. Jonathan wrapped his arms around his son, and hugged him tightly.

"I missed you too, Daddy," the boy confessed.

Jonathan rested his chin on the top of the child's head, inhaled the pure, innocent scent of his freshly-washed hair. "I'm sorry to have stayed away so long," he said. "But I'm home for good now. No more mean Uncle Andrew, I promise."

This seemed to satisfy Jon-Jon. His thumb went immediately into his mouth, and he leaned his head on his father's shoulder. Sarina looked only slightly mollified.

"What happened to Uncle Michael?" She asked.

Jonathan was surprised to feel discomfited by the question. After all, he was not so clueless as to expect they might never ask. Sarina and Jon-Jon had been close to their Uncle Michael, and children are curious creatures by nature. His and Stella's children were no exceptions, but—fortunately for Jonathan—children could also be easily misled.

He thought his uneasiness might be due to something he hadn't factored into the equation during the many sleepless nights he'd spent thinking about how he was going to explain Michael's absence: Jonathan had forgotten how vivid and intense Sarina's gaze could be. It was more than a little disconcerting to look into his daughter's eyes, and feel as though he were peering into the soul of an ancient diviner masquerading as a five-year-old girl.

"Uncle Michael was very sick," He began, careful to keep his voice even and emotionless, so she wouldn't sense the lie. "The doctors tried everything they could to help him, but nothing worked. Uncle Michael is in heaven with Momma now."

"That's not what Andrew Simon said," Sarina replied. "Before you came upstairs, I heard you arguing in the library, and he said it's all your fault that Michael is wandering lost in the Shadowlands. He said, 'If you would have stopped Michael from going to Blackwater Hills, none of it would have ever happened.' So, if Uncle Michael is lost, that means he isn't really dead. Right, Daddy?"

"I'm sorry, Sarina. I wish he were still alive as much as you do, but I can assure you, Uncle Michael is not coming back."

Her chin jutted out at a stubborn angle. She planted her hands on her hips, narrowed her eyes, and glared at him.

"That means that one of you is lying."

Called out by a five-year-old girl. His own daughter, no less. Jonathan shifted uncomfortably, adjusting his son's weight. He avoided his daughter's gaze as he tried to come up with a way to explain away what she had overheard, without coming right out and confessing the whole sordid, ugly truth.

He did not want Sarina and Jon-Jon to know what had really happened to Michael. Jonathan was prepared to do much worse than lie in order to ensure that his children never learned from what madness they had been descended. If it was the last thing he ever did, he would make sure they never set foot in the miles of shielded forest known as Blackwater Hills.

It's for their own good, he reminded himself, and so delivered the lines as calmly and delicately as he could.

"Neither of us is lying, sweetheart. Andrew Simon and I were discussing the plot of my latest novel, not Uncle Michael. I'm sorry you misinterpreted what you heard, I truly am. I would never lie to you, Sarina. Uncle Michael is dead."

The mask slipped, revealing the vulnerability she always seemed so desperate to hide. Sarina's eyes filled with unshed tears, and suddenly she was a little girl again. A lonely, confused little girl who had lost both her mother and her favorite uncle in the span of two short years.

Jonathan felt a stirring of guilt for his selfishness, for staying away so long, for not being there to give his children what they deserved—his love and attention, some semblance of their former life. But parenting was not his forte. Never had been. Stella had always made it seem so effortless.

He reached out with his free hand, and beckoned her over. She hesitated for a moment, then crossed the room and fell into his one-armed embrace. He sat for a long time, holding his children close, wishing he could change the past, and desperately hoping he was capable of protecting them from whatever the future had in store.

Dusk seeped through the sheer white curtains, cloaking the room in shadow. Jon-Jon's breathing gradually grew softer, and Sarina's small body relaxed, slightly. He eased his son under the covers, then carried his daughter down the long hallway to her bedroom. He buried her up to her neck in the fluffy, white comforter, then leaned down and lightly kissed the top of her forehead.

"Sleep tight, sweetheart," he whispered. "I will see you in the morning."

She nodded sleepily, rolled over, and closed her eyes.

Jonathan left the bedroom, and headed downstairs to the library. Once ensconced behind his desk, he began sorting through the veritable mountain of mail piled precariously atop it.

Light bill. Gas bill. Phone bill seriously past due and warning him in large, bold letters that this would be his final notice before service was terminated. A stack of drugstore sympathy cards from friends and acquaintances offering insincere, meaningless condolences.

When he came to a book-sized package wrapped in plain brown paper, he hesitated, hands arrested in midair. His name and address had been inked across the top in a flowing, feminine script he had never seen before, yet recognized instantly. There was no return address.

Sweat broke out on his forehead and under his arms. He was overcome by the chilling certainty that he should just pick up the package and toss it straight into the garbage, for surely, whatever was inside had the power to tear open wounds that had not fully healed.

Against his better judgment—stomach in knots, and heart pounding—Jonathan lifted the package and tore it open. A folded sheet of yellow parchment paper slid onto the desk. He tossed the wrapping aside, and stared at the object in his hands: a well-used notebook, cover creased and smudged with dirt, the corners of the pages stained and dog-eared. He peeled back the cover, recognized his own clumsy, awkward scrawl:

Property of: Jonathan Lance Sr.
1154 Sheridan Road
Ashland, ME 04732

He took a deep, calming breath, and—as though it were a trap ready to spring at the slightest touch—gingerly turned the page and began to read:

March 19
Somewhere in the North Maine Woods

Michael swears we're not lost, but I'm not sure I believe him.

Why did I let him talk me into this? Doors to the Otherworld? What a load of crap.

Aside from that, it's beautiful here. The roar of the mighty Blackwater River bounces off the mountains and echoes through the valley. The air tastes thin, and crackles with static. The smells of rotting leaves, rich earth, and fragrant pine are overpowering. I'm trying to, as Michael says, listen for the heartbeat of the forest—all the while thinking how silly it is to imagine that such a thing actually exists. What's even sillier, is imagining that if it did exist, I'd be able to hear it. Not I, the great novelist J. Lance Sr..

Otherwise known as the most normal man in the world, as Stella had been so fond of saying.

So, I'm trying to think of this adventure in terms of a novel. The opening might go something like this:

"And now we bring you the incredible adventures of Normal Man and his sidekick, Werewolf Boy! Watch as they spend countless hours trudging through the wilderness. You'll be on the edge of your seat as Normal Man feels absolutely nothing, while Werewolf Boy looks as though he's going to lose it any second."

Then again...

Perhaps not.

A review of my sketchy knowledge of the Singleton family, from the oldest to the youngest:
Branden Singleton (Michael's father)
Stella Singleton (My wife)
Andrew Simon Singleton

Jared Singleton
Jackson Singleton

    Nine years ago, I married my soul mate, the most beautiful woman I have ever known. Her name was Stella Singleton. She came with baggage—namely, her thirteen year-old nephew, Michael, whose father had passed away the previous year. Back then, Michael was a quiet, confused young man who had been traumatized by his father's death, so I tried my best to be both father and friend—first to the boy, then to the man. Now that Stella is gone, I feel that I must continue to watch over her beloved nephew.

    But I'm sure there must be a sane, logical explanation for Michael's peculiar malady. People do not go around changing into wolves. They never have, and they never will.

March 20
Still Have No Idea Where the Hell We Are

    Michael has informed me that we are due to arrive in Blackwater Hills during the spring solstice celebration when the tribe celebrates the birthday of Tempus, the god of Time. As we sat round our campfire last night, he recounted a bit of the legend for me, which I will transcribe here to ensure I remember all of it:

    Sol and Luna, God and Goddess of the sun and the moon, Father and Mother of the heavens and the earth, joined as one and gave birth to four children. First born was Fatum, the god of Fate. Second born was Tempus, the god of Time. Third born was

Venefica, the Witch of the Shadowlands, and last born was Corvus, the Beast of the Otherworld.

Tempus ruled the lives of humans, but was a strict parent, easily offended, and slow to forgive. She liked to control Her children by holding the promise of eternity just out of reach, threatening to withdraw it in an instant if they did not behave according to Her dictates.

Fatum had no children of his own, but was a caring, somewhat enigmatic uncle who aided his siblings' offspring in times of crisis.

Venefica the Witch had many children; some shared human blood, and some did not. The Witch favored daughters above sons, much the way Corvus gave His greatest gifts to His male children. But Venefica and Her daughters craved even more power, and grew jealous and resentful over the years.

The Witch imprisoned her brother, Corvus, and attempted to drain His shapeshifting power. Corvus managed to escape, but the act turned brother and sister from allies to enemies. To this day, Venefica and Corvus remain bitter rivals, which is why the children of Corvus must always be wary of the advena.

10:21 am
We Are Finally Fucking Here

I've decided that Jackson Singleton (Michael's paternal uncle, and my wife's youngest brother) resembles neither Michael, Stella, nor her brother, Andrew Simon. The other three were dark-haired and golden-skinned, like Native Americans. Jackson's light brown hair hangs like a wet bed sheet on either side his lean face. He is at least as tall as Michael (six feet, four inches), but about forty pounds lighter, with narrow shoulders and limbs that seem too long in proportion to his torso.

Jackson's shocked expression borders on comical. He sits at a square, plank table surrounded by four rickety stools. Michael's large body is balanced awkwardly atop the stool closest to the door. I'm sitting at the head of the table, trying to make sense of their strange and stilted conversation, while at the same time wondering if shock might be Jackson's natural expression; his homely face seems to favor it more than any other.

The cabin is sparsely furnished in a style that can best be described as fashionably rustic, owing to the actual use of the myriad antique tools cluttering the walls and furniture. Not, I am sure, because Jackson gives any thought whatsoever to the way his home is decorated. The main room consists of a kitchen and small dining room, while an open doorway on the left leads into a tiny, windowless alcove that serves as the sleeping quarters. The entire cabin cannot measure more than five hundred square feet, and I am disappointed to find nothing that even remotely resembles a bathroom.

Jackson says, "Be honest, Michael. You are my brother's son. After the tragedy that nearly destroyed our family, the last thing I want to see, is another Singleton male spill his blood upon the altar of Tempus."

Goosebumps rise on the skin of my forearms. Don't ask me why.

Almost imperceptibly, Michael's broad shoulders stiffen. "There's nothing to worry about, Jackson. I have it under control."

I discover that Jackson's expression can change, as it warps to incorporate incredulity.

"Are you certain?" He asks.

Michael nods. "Absolutely."

6:07 pm
Waxing Introspective During the Solstice

When I reluctantly agreed to accompany Michael on this fool's errand—excuse me, Journey to his Homeland—I'd felt as though coming to Blackwater Hills would somehow bring me closer to Stella, keep her alive in my thoughts, here with me the only way she could be. But now, as I imagine her sitting in this very spot year after year—belonging to this mysterious tribe of Native American /Druid/ Werewolf people–I realize there was a huge part of my wife that I had never even known, had never even suspected was there.

Outside in the clearing on the rise of the hill, a bonfire rages in a deep, circular pit lined with heavy, flat rocks. Surrounding the pit are benches made from thick tree trunks, laid out in rows like a makeshift stadium. I cast surreptitious glances at the people seated round the bonfire, noting how their eyes seem to follow my progress, and it occurs to me that perhaps I am more unwelcome at this gathering than Jackson's prodigal nephew.

Michael warned me that the tribe does not take kindly to outsiders. They even have a name for me: Advena. It means, "Outsider."

Thus far, I have only heard it spoken in a less-than-flattering manner.

Because of this, I am talking only when spoken to—mostly neutral and, I hope, universal platitudes. However, it's not every day that a fantasy writer gets the opportunity to observe a clan of pseudo-druids celebrate the spring solstice. The experience could prove invaluable, for research purposes. I tell myself to quit worrying about things I know nothing about, relax, and not take everything so goddamn seriously.

Lighten up, Normal Man.

What's the worst that can happen?

CHAPTER ONE
Alena Speaks

Alena Andrick
Blackwater Hills

Eight separate families comprised the tribe of Corvus. At last count, we numbered over a thousand. And by the looks of things, most of those had shown up at the castle for the *Vernus*. Late on the afternoon of the sacred celebration, I arrived to find my usually quiet home bursting its mortar with relatives and friends. The ceremonial bonfire raged in the massive firepit outside, but the icy March wind had, apparently, blown everyone indoors.

I passed through the crowded entryway into the Great Hall, winding my way through the people occupied in games and conversation at the long, plank tables. The cavernous kitchen was nearly as crowded. Women darted about in an efficient, choreographed dance. Some fed the fire in the woodstove, while others stirred the steaming pots on top. Sayla Kendrick bent over the oven, poking its contents with a long-handled fork. Others stood alongside the narrow sideboard, slicing food and arranging it neatly on platters. My mother stood by the sink, pumping water from the creaky, old faucet. Her massive bosom heaved with the effort beneath her homemade tunic.

When she finally glanced up and saw me hiding in the doorway, she stopped pumping and fixed me with an exasperated glare. "Nice of you to join us, Alena. Where have you been all morning?"

"Practicing spells. The final exam is less than a month away, and if I fail, I'll have to do the whole course over. *Again.*"

"Well, I suppose it's better late than never. Come on in and hang up your cloak. I could use another set of hands."

Reluctantly, I threaded my way through the maze of bodies, and added my cloak to the mound balanced precariously on a long row of cast iron hooks by the basement door. Out of the corner of my eye, I saw Kira MacDonald lean over a stack of firewood and whisper something to the girl next to her. Fifteen year-old Nela Alexander slanted a glance at me, then giggled beneath her hand. Kira smirked in my direction, and elbowed her conspirator in the ribs. My cheeks warmed with anger, or embarrassment—I wasn't quite sure which. My mother turned around just in time to witness the exchange. A frown creased the skin between her liquid brown eyes.

"I see you made an effort to dress for the occasion," she remarked as I approached the sink.

I sighed inwardly. *Here we go again.*

My flannel shirt was worn, but clean. A few sizes too large, it puffed around my waist like a lumpy sack of grain. My tall leather boots were scuffed and worn, and there was a tear in the fabric of my trousers, just below my right knee. My outfit was well-suited for practicing spells in the forest, but—to my never-ending consternation—a celebration such as the

Vernus required a bit more attention to tedious details like clothing and manners.

"You know I don't have any dresses, Mother," I answered. "Pants are more comfortable, anyway."

"It wouldn't hurt to brush your hair," Mother advised, handing me a towel and a freshly washed platter.

I shrugged, set the dried plate aside, and picked up the next one. "I can't help that it's windy outside."

"Well, the feast is nearly ready, anyway. Go on upstairs, and fix yourself up. *Honestly,* Alena. You're so pretty. Would it kill you to show it off once in a while?"

I dropped the towel on the counter, and glanced pointedly at Kira. "I don't really care what they say about me, Mother."

"Well, you should," my mother replied. "They're your own people, not strangers. Family is everything. *No man is an island.*"

Mother was always repeating little phrases like that. She had a list somewhere, of all the quotes she had copied from books. She said they inspired her to think and be a better person. Apparently, she hoped they'd do the same for me. Grateful for any excuse to get out of the kitchen, I squared my shoulders and tried to adopt an air of serene but confident detachment.

I'll survive being stared at and whispered about, I thought as exited the kitchen through the Great Hall. *I always do.*

Still, what I'd said to Mother had been a lie. Though I couldn't explain why, I did care what they said about me. I just wasn't sure what to do about it, because it seemed like an incredible waste of time to fuss over my appearance. What difference could it possibly make to anyone?

Just inside the entryway, I was jolted from my musings by the sight of a tall, black—haired stranger sprawled on the bench by the fireplace. Like a lazy cat waking from an afternoon nap, the stranger tilted his head to one side and blinked slowly.

My appreciative gaze traveled over scuffed black leather boots crossed at the ankles, his long legs stretched toward the fire, muscular limbs and broad shoulders, finally coming to rest on a face that looked to have been molded in the image of some ancient deity. Firelight warmed his smooth, tanned skin, while flames flickered and danced with the shadows in his eyes.

His gaze met mine, and I swallowed, hard. For the second time in less than a quarter hour, I felt my cheeks burn with embarrassment. Social customs were not my strong suit. How could they be, after all, when I spent the majority of my time alone? Without speaking a word to acknowledge his presence, I fled up the winding stone staircase to the third floor of the tower. Once safely ensconced in my bedchamber, I found a hairbrush buried beneath the pile of books and scrolls that littered the dresser. As I worked out the tangles in my waist—long hair, I stared at my reflection in the dusty mirror.

I sometimes didn't recognize myself. It seemed, sometimes, as though the person staring back through the mirror wasn't really me. Inside, I felt much stronger than this frail body suggested, more cunning than this innocent visage might imply. Everyone assumed that I preferred tomes and scrolls to flesh and spirit, and so left me to my own devices. No one ever seemed to take me seriously, and I was pretty sure it was because the sweet young girl in the mirror looked boring and harmless.

I fished in my pockets for the leather thong I always carried. After tying my hair into a loose knot atop my head, I pulled the long tail of my shirt out of the waistband of my trousers, but when I stepped back to examine the results, was less than pleased. I looked, I thought hopelessly, like a little girl playing dress-up in her brother's old clothing.

Unfortunately, that was as good as it was likely to get. My wardrobe consisted primarily of flannel shirts and trousers exactly like the ones I was already wearing. The only variations were in color and state of disrepair, because I hated to sew about as much as I hated doing laundry.

When I came back downstairs, the entryway was empty, and the beautiful stranger was gone from the hearthside. Mother emerged from the kitchen, two large platters stacked with meats, cheeses, rolls, and fruit balanced precariously on the palms of her hands. Her eyes softened when she noticed my halfhearted attempt at improving my appearance.

"Go on in and sit down, Alena. Our table is the one all the way in back, against the wall."

She led me through the maze of tables, chairs, and bodies. I slid into an empty seat at the far end of a table painted with the crest of the Maxwells—even though, technically, I wasn't one of them. Enticing scents wafted through the archway as the women brought in platter after platter of food. My stomach growled in anticipation. Eventually the streams of women and platters ran dry, and everyone took their seats. My father stood upon the dais to recite the blessing, and the steady murmur of voices faded to contemplative silence.

"Corvus protect us," he began, his voice lilting and musical, like water trickling down a rocky hillside. "On this day, the birthday of your beloved sister, *Tempus,* bless us Father, and hear our prayer. Guide us with the wisdom of your Sacred Law, so one day we might join you in the glory of the Otherworld. We know that the Law of Corvus is truth. The truth is sacred."

"The Law of Corvus is truth. The truth is sacred," the crowd replied in unison.

Someone coughed. Chair legs scraped against the smooth stone floor. Father sat down at the head of the table reserved for priests of the Sacred Order, and the gentle hum of conversation resumed. I watched my Father with the other priests at the table, laughing, smiling, and nodding his head, engrossed by what they had to say. So different from the way he looked at me — with that cloudy, bemused expression that implied he thought me little more than an irritating distraction.

Someday soon I'll be sitting at that table. He'll notice me then, I'll bet.

I was jarred from my musings by Mother, who leaned over my shoulder to plunk a good-sized serving of mashed potatoes on my plate. I thanked her with a nod, then watched as she took her seat at one end of the table.

At the head of the table, opposite Mother, sat the Captain of the Guard, Innes Maxwell. My mother's *lifemate* looked disgruntled and unapproachable, as usual. To his left sat Seamus MacDonald and his younger brother, Ian. Next to Ian, was the *Medicus,*

Jackson Singleton. To Innes's right sat his son, my half-brother, Donnall Maxwell. Donnall's *lifemate* Shaina was by his side, deep in conversation with Sayla Kendrick. I scanned the remainder of the seats to see if Elise Kendrick, Sayla's daughter had arrived yet, and my heart gave a little leap of surprise when I saw who was next to Sayla, diagonally across the table from me.

It was the beautiful stranger who'd been reclining by the fireplace earlier. Next to him was someone else I didn't recognize. This man was older, lean and wiry, and had the fragile look of a human about him. His bright blue eyes drooped beneath the weight of dark, unruly eyebrows. His nose was broad, almost too large for his face. He whispered something in the beautiful stranger's ear, revealing a row of even white teeth, like thick pieces of chalk.

It was odd to see an *advena* sitting at the Maxwell's table, so near Innes, who made no secret of his hate and distrust of humans. We'd had occasional outside visitors to our celebrations over the years, but the Sacred Law of Corvus cautioned against bringing the *advena* through the Great Shield too often. Subtle nuances were lost on the Captain of the Guard, but Innes appeared to be tolerating the human's presence for the moment.

The same could not be said for my half-brother. Beneath a shaggy mane of brown hair, Donnall's glare alternated slowly back and forth between the human and the black-haired stranger. The stranger appeared not to notice, but the human shifted in his seat, looking ill at ease.

The stranger acknowledged my perusal with a wicked, close-mouthed grin that made my stomach quiver. His lips—full, sensual, utterly masculine—curled up slightly in a private smile, causing me to wonder at the source of his amusement. His hands rested on the table, fingers entwined as though in prayer. He had strong, capable hands. Scarred and rough-looking, but with an unexpected hint of elegance.

Good looks aren't everything, I hurried to remind myself. You can never tell what might be lurking beneath the surface. He could be abusive, controlling. Or, even more frightening, unintelligent. He could, in fact, already be joined with another woman. A man like that didn't stay unmated for long, even with the aforementioned flaws. Some women were willing to tolerate certain faults in exchange for the security of a *lifemate.* If nothing else, he'd make gorgeous children.

"Your hair is beautiful," he said. His voice was deep and rough, like the soft growl of thunder on a summer afternoon. "I never realized that tribal blood could produce such glorious colors."

I blushed clear down to the tips of my toes. And for someone with my *glorious coloring,* I knew it was glaringly obvious. I'd inherited my red-gold hair and pale skin from my father, Claudius. *A throwback to the German,* they said of Claudius and me, for we favored our human ancestors over those of the tanned skinned, black-haired children of Corvus.

"Gratiae," I mumbled, and quickly grabbed the heaping platter of venison Mother was offering me. I plunked a few slices onto my plate, then passed the meat to Shaina.

Ian MacDonald bit off a chunk of bread, and waved the half-eaten slice in the air. "I used to call her 'Alena the *advena'* when we were kids," he remarked, spewing crumbs down the front of his shirt. "Until she turned about twelve, and then she threatened to cut off my balls if I ever called her that again."

Shaina giggled. Mother slanted me a glance and raised her eyebrows.

"Well, it worked," I mumbled. "He never did."

Ian grinned sheepishly. "I half—believed she would do it, too!"

"She's Andrick's get. Spoilt with the blood of *Tempus,"* Donnall interjected.

An uncomfortable silence settled over the table. Even Innes managed to look shocked by his son's bluntness. Everyone at the table glanced at me, then quickly looked away.

"You, on the other hand..." Donnall studied the black—haired stranger through narrowed eyes. Then, as though stating the obvious, said, "The Singletons never did manage to breed the curse from their blood, but I don't need to tell you that. Do I, Michael?"

The stranger's nostrils flared, like an animal scenting prey. He said nothing in reply, as he reached for his cask of wine and raised it to his lips.

Donnall smirked and gestured toward Michael's wine cask. "You've always had the luck of a *daemon,* Singleton, but maybe you should have stayed in the land of the *advena,* cause your luck's bound to run out sooner or later. My bet's on sooner. Like tomorrow, for instance. Soon as the vintner locks up his stores."

The stranger made a sound suspiciously like a growl, low in his throat, but Donnall continued, apparently warming to the subject. "Here's a little piece of advice: be careful not to stand too close to the firepit. There's always the chance you might *accidentally* fall in."

Jackson stood up hurriedly, knocking over his chair. A hush fell over the cavernous Great Hall. "That's quite enough!" he ordered, sounding like a schoolmaster reprimanding an unruly pupil. "I suggest you quit while you're ahead, Donnall."

Donnall rolled his eyes. "Forgive me, Honorable *Medicus,*" he begged, sounding not in the least humbled. "I forgot how sensitive you Singletons can be."

"Parvi refert," Jackson replied after a long, tense moment. He bent to retrieve his overturned chair. No one at our table said a word as he righted it, and resumed his seat. Donnall's green eyes glittered—with something more than a reflection of the torchlight, it seemed to me.

Alarmed, I glanced from Michael to Donnall. The expression on my half-brother's face made my blood run cold. I knew that look. As the only child of the Guardian of the Dead—and training to be a priestess, to boot—it would be remiss of me to not notice.

Donnall was a member of the Guard, not a priest of the Sacred Order. Nevertheless, he had the look of a priest performing *captare.* Glittering eyes, that faint, greenish glow to his skin. His aura shimmered and appeared to rise up, as though his body was becoming lighter than air.

I looked helplessly around the table, struck by an overwhelming urge to *do* something. Protect Michael, somehow. No one else seemed to have picked up on what Donnall was doing, and would probably not have interfered, if they had. Before I had a chance to consider the consequences, I closed my eyes and gathered in my power.

It had taken years of practice to learn to ascend to the Balance, but I was now able to do it in a matter of seconds. The warm, white-gold glow of magic tingled through every nerve in my body. I silently chanted the prayer for protection, then erected a seamless, impenetrable shield around my soul and mortal body.

Corvus protect your servant who dwells within this shield. Let no one breach this barrier by thought or deed.

The spell was one I'd been practicing that morning. The fact that I had not yet perfected the much simpler version, a shield that would protect only myself, did not deter me. Once in place, the shield thickened and pulsed like a silent heartbeat. Slowly, carefully, I reached out—as though my mind had a thousand invisible hands—and widened the shield to include Michael Singleton.

A surge of raw power struck me like a bolt of lightning. The shield began to disintegrate rapidly. I heard a loud buzzing in my ears. My body felt numb, and pinpricks of light danced before my eyes.

Stop! A voice inside my head commanded. *You have nothing left. Let me take over.*

I was so shocked by the invasion of my mind, I let go of my tentative hold on the shield. When I realized my mistake, panic took over, freezing the breath in my lungs. I braced for the inevitable agony that followed making a too-rapid descent. Unpleasant did not even begin to describe it. I wasn't very good at dealing with pain, and someone was sure to notice if I passed out cold in the middle of a feast.

But the pain didn't come. As though from a long ways away, I heard Mother ask a question about the previous winter's supply of candles. The formidable Sayla Kendrick was not one to pass up an opportunity to captivate an audience, and began recounting the trials and tribulations inherent in her position as chandler. She reminded everyone it was a sin to be wasteful, not to mention it made her job a million times harder.

If I was going to pass out, it would have happened by now. I took a deep breath, relieved that my lungs seemed to again be working properly, then slanted a glance at Michael through lowered lashes. A dimple flashed in his cheek as he cut off a chunk of meat, brought it to his mouth, and chewed slowly.

What on earth did you think you were doing?

The intrusion was not so shocking the second time, but it was strange to hear his voice in my mind. The ability to transmit thoughts so clearly was rare, a skill very few priests were capable of. I avoided looking at him, picked up my fork and toyed idly with the mound of mashed potatoes on my plate. Though I wasn't sure he'd be able to hear me, I answered in the same manner:

Protecting you.

Deep, masculine laughter echoed inside my head.

It's not funny, I replied, bristling at the ingratitude. *Donnall was... Looking.*

When there was no reply, I glanced up. Michael was frowning, studying Donnall. But Donnall, engaged in a full—out assault on his food, seemed to have completely lost interest in Michael. Michael's full lips tightened in a grim line, and a muscle jumped inside his jaw. The shield still pulsed around us, and a quick glance around the table assured me that everyone seemed to be effectively distracted by it.

Michael reached across the table, grabbed his cask of ceremonial wine, and drank deeply. His gaze met mine, and I had the oddest sensation, like I was sliding down a mountain toward the edge of a tall cliff. Then Michael blinked, and the sensation vanished.

Gratiae, Alena. I owe you one.

* ~ * ~ *

The winds calmed as the sun began to sink below the ring of white—capped mountains in the distance. Gradually people stood and dispersed, making their way outside where they assembled around the massive bonfire. The tribe began to chant the traditional verses. I took a seat on one of the large logs laid out around the firepit, and mouthed the words along with rest. Though most of us had imbibed more than our share of ceremonial wine, the sacred chants were so ingrained in our collective consciousness, even the influence of drink could not dislodge them.

A gathering was one of only four times per cycle that members of the tribe of Corvus (excluding the Guard and the Sacred Order, who were allowed supervised access throughout the year) were permitted to drink their fill. The rest of the time, the wine was strictly off-limits, for it was known to cause dependency and sickness in some. I raised a half-empty cask to my lips, sipped at the tangy, bitter concoction, felt it burn its way down my throat and settle in my stomach. Then I lowered the cask to my knees, and looked around.

My gaze was immediately drawn to Michael. There was an aura of readiness about him, a wary, hunted look in his midnight eyes. Wedged between the *advena* and Jackson Singleton, he was clad in a pair of threadbare jeans, black leather boots, and a blue flannel shirt with the sleeves rolled up over muscular forearms. A black wool cloak draped his broad shoulders. Stubble darkened the lower portion of his jaw, and tousled waves of dark hair tumbled over his forehead.

I could still feel the shield pulsing around me, but could no longer hear Michael's voice in my mind. The spell seemed to be gradually growing weaker, and I wondered what might happen when Michael let go of it altogether. Would I suffer a delayed reaction to the shock of descending too fast from the Balance? Did Michael suspect that might be the case? Why else would he still be holding on to the shield?

Jarred from my musings by a light tap on my shoulder from behind, I turned my head to see Elise Kendrick smiling brightly down at me. Silky, black hair framed her perfect, oval face, contrasting sharply with her creamy pale skin. At five feet eleven inches, slender and long-legged, her every movement was as graceful as a willow in the wind.

"Scoot over," she said, lifting one leg over the log and settling down next to me.

"Where've you been?" I asked. "I didn't see you at the feast."

She grimaced. "The first day of my moontime, I can barely even make it out of bed. I'm feeling a little better now, but the last thing I want to do is celebrate. Naturally, the one and only time something interesting happens, I wasn't there. I can't believe I missed Donnall's freak-out."

I smiled, knowing that had to be just about killing her. "It was one of his better ones. Guaranteed to be retold for gatherings-to-come."

She pouted. "Don't rub it in. Kira told me what happened."

For one, fleeting instant I considered confiding in Elise about my failed attempt to shield Michael. She was like an older sister to me, after all. She actually paid attention to the things I said, even looked genuinely interested most of the time. But for all her obvious perfection, Elise had a major flaw in her character: she loved to gossip. With a mother like Sayla, I supposed it was inevitable.

Given that, I decided to keep my secret to myself, for the time being. We basked in the warm glow of the bonfire in companionable silence, and after a while, my gaze wandered back to Michael. He was deep in conversation with the *advena*—Jonathan, I'd heard him called—and didn't seem to notice me at all. Elise's gaze soon traveled the same path.

"He's been gone a long time," she said, sounding as though she was talking more to herself than to me. "I wonder why he came back."

I assumed she was talking about Michael. "Where did he go?" I asked.

"To the land of the *advena*. His aunt and uncle took him away about ten years ago. He's maybe a year or so older than me, so he might have been around twelve or thirteen."

Well, that explained why I didn't recognize him. If Michael was one year older than Elise, I would have been only nine years old when he left the tribe.

"He sat behind me in class, and used to pull on my braids during Ivan's lessons," she went on, grinning at the memory. "He was awfully cute, though, so I never got mad at him. You were lucky to have Simon Kendrick for a teacher, Alena. Ivan's lectures were so *boring.*"

"Why'd they take him away?" I wondered aloud.

Elise's eyes widened. "You mean you don't *know?*"

"Know what?"

"Oh, Alena," she admonished. "You're always the last to know everything."

"Know what?" I repeated. "Stop smirking, and tell me."

"It's a long story," she said. "I'll tell you later. Did you hear that Shaina's due in October?"

"Shaina's pregnant *again?*" I exclaimed. "Donnall doesn't waste any time, does he?"

Elise looked annoyed. "Makes you sick, doesn't it? She's on her third, and I haven't even had one yet."

"Motherhood's not all it's built up to be," I said, trying to make her feel better. "I hear it hurts. A lot."

She sighed—a gentle, wistful sound. "Some rewards are worth the pain, Alena."

"I guess." I shrugged, willing to concede the point. After all, it wasn't like I knew from personal experience. Most girls my age had *lifemates,* or children of their own to care for. I had neither, and was beginning to suspect that unless a miracle happened, I never would.

Elise stood up abruptly. *"Gods,* I almost forgot. Tarren wants me to help him get ready for the sacrifice to *Tempus.* He said a lot more people are doing it this year, and everyone thinks they should be allowed to go first. The arguing got so bad, they decided to pick names out of a hat. Tarren volunteered *me* to be the one to keep track of the order."

She wrinkled her delicate, turned-up nose. "I swear, that man expects me to work every gathering, just because he has to. Are you doing the sacrifice?"

I shook my head no. Elise and Tarren Campbell, a young priest newly sworn to the Sacred Order, had joined as *lifemates* two summers ago. Since then, Elise never seemed to have time for me. I missed her. Despite our age difference, we had always been close. She had spent many nights at the castle when I was a little girl, and we used to stay awake till dawn, talking and acting silly.

A part of me yearned for things to be that way still, and I made no effort to hide my disappointment. "I guess I'll see you later, then. Maybe."

She flashed me an apologetic smile, then disappeared back into the crowd. I took another swig out of my nearly empty cask of wine, and decided I needed to use the privy. On my way out, I stopped just inside the opened castle door, and took in the sight on the rise of the hillside. Though I couldn't see him from where I was standing, I thought of Michael, wondered how he felt coming back here after so many years spent living in the human world.

As I watched the tribe revel in the celebration, a heavy sense of melancholy settled over me. These people were my family, all I'd ever known, but still, somewhere deep down inside, I felt as though I didn't belong. I didn't feel the same sense of oneness everyone else seemed to feel, and couldn't explain why.

I wondered if maybe there was something lacking in me, if I had been born with some sort of emotional deficiency. Then again, it could be I just didn't try hard enough. I wasn't really sure what to do about that. Should I march back into the midst of the festivities and start chattering merrily with everyone—like Kira MacDonald and her group of feather-headed busybodies? What would people think? They'd think I was either crazed or drunk on ceremonial wine, most likely. Maybe a gathering wasn't the best time to try and improve my inadequate social skills.

I'd much rather practice spells, instead. I stepped onto the stone path that wound around to the back of the castle, crossed the meadow, and slipped into the forest. The air felt moist and cool, and smelled like rain. Mice and chipmunks skittered through leaves and underbrush, and from somewhere deep inside the forest, an owl hooted. It was a sound of profound, yet resigned, loneliness.

I prepared to center my power by breathing in deeply, then exhaling slowly. But as I approached my favorite practice spot—a small clearing surrounding the remains of what had once been a majestic pine tree—my stomach turned queasy, my vision blurred, and I felt a throbbing in my temples that promised to blossom into a full-fledged pounding. The pattern of my footsteps on the spongy forest floor sounded unusually loud. The noise lingered in the air, blending with the strange, rhythmic humming that was swallowing everything. The forest melted away, and a soft light enveloped me, like a tingling, white coverlet.

Disembodied, I floated inside...

CHAPTER TWO
Secrets and Lies

Alena Andrick
Blackwater Hills

I came to awareness on the soggy forest floor. The scent of rotting leaves invaded my nose. The whir of locusts assaulted my ears. The gibbous moon hanging low in the sky outlined a hulking black shadow mere inches from my face. A startled scream lodged in my throat.

"Relax," said the shadow. "It's only me."

Relief supplanted fear as I recognized the distinctive, husky timbre of his voice. It was Michael Singleton. He must have spotted me leaving the celebration, and followed me here.

I shook my head to clear the cloudy, cobwebby feeling, and managed to sit up. The ground tilted, and my stomach roiled in sickening rebellion. Michael leaned in to help, but I instinctively recoiled. A heartbeat later, the underbrush rustled as he moved away.

When my eyes adjusted to the moonlit dark, the hulking black shadow transformed into a face and body too gorgeous to be real. He reclined against the trunk of the fallen pine tree, one arm draped casually over his knee. Goosebumps rose on my forearms, and excitement danced with apprehension in the pit of my belly.

Gods, no one can be that handsome. There has to be a flaw somewhere.

"You should have been expecting that, Alena. It was reckless and foolish, running off by yourself."

I bristled at the scolding, but had to admit, he was right. I should have realized the shield would fade sooner, rather than later, leaving me vulnerable to the negative effect of my failed spellcraft during supper. Which, by all appearances, is exactly what ended up happening. I was grateful to Michael for coming to my rescue, but the attention made me feel awkward and oddly unsure of myself.

"Yeah well, so was trying to shield you, and that didn't stop me."

He grunted agreement. "May I ask *why* you did it?"

"It seemed like a good idea at the time," I muttered, rubbing my aching forehead.

His low chuckle echoed a faraway rumble of thunder. "For what it's worth, the same applies to me, but I never imagined Donnall would nurse a grudge for ten years."

I recalled their confrontation during dinner—which hadn't actually made sense to me at the time. It made even less sense now, in my befuddled state. However, it didn't really seem like the right time to question Michael about why he and Donnall were at odds with each other.

"He's my brother," I said. "Well, *half*-brother, actually."

Michael looked puzzled. "I thought he said you were an Andrick?"

I saw him frown as understanding dawned. Ours was the smallest family in the tribe. There were not, after all, many Andricks left, and only one logical choice to have fathered a child of nineteen winters.

"The Guardian of the Dead is your *father?"*

"Yeah," I said, attempting to stand up. "I'm his only child. Cora Maxwell is my mother, but she and my father aren't *lifemates.* She mated with Innes, Donnall's father, and they live together in a cabin north of the castle, along the river's edge. I grew up with my father and grandfather in the castle, so I could train to join the Sacred Order and take over the Guardianship when he's ready to step down."

The news appeared to distress him, though I didn't immediately make the connection. My head was pounding a slow, steady rhythm against my temples, and when I tried to take a step forward, the ground undulated beneath me like a storm-swollen lake. I tumbled headfirst into the underbrush. Moments later, I felt strong arms encircle my waist like iron bands. Michael untangled me from the clinging vines, placing a hand beneath my elbow to steady me.

"Steady, Alena. Deep, even breaths," he instructed. "The dizziness will pass soon, but don't try to stand by yourself, yet. Lean on me."

Michael was an exceptionally tall man. Close as he was, he felt as solid and immobile as the tree against my back. Thunder rumbled, sounding far away. The wind returned, gusting through the leaves, whipping my long hair over my eyes.

He reached out, gently brushed the errant strands away from my face. My wary gaze followed the well-defined curve of his jaw, traced the hollows and angles of his high cheekbones and perfectly sculpted nose.

When I reached his eyes, my heart skipped a beat, and my palms began to sweat, despite the chilly night air. I couldn't help but be seduced by the passion in those midnight eyes. It was as though his soul—too intense for the limitations of mortality—was fighting to escape the confines of his body.

I breathed in the scent of musky male, as his fingers smoothed my tangled hair. I leaned into the hard wall of his chest, and he lowered his head. His lips touched mine, ever so gently, and my heart threatened to burst through my ribcage. Then he lifted his head, ending the kiss, leaving me hollow, empty, wanting more.

"Come with me, Alena. There's something I want to show you."

"No," I managed, my voice sounding weak and breathless. He inhaled sharply, as though the denial had wounded him.

"Please, my love," he coaxed in a dark, husky whisper that hummed through my nerve-endings. *"Fatum* brought us together for a reason, and one should never defy the will of a god."

I was, after all, the daughter of a priest, and incapable of resisting any sort of theological debate. "One should never be so presumptuous as to think he, alone, discerns the god's will," I countered. "Haven't you ever heard the old adage, *Pride goeth before a fall?"*

"Too late," he murmured. "I've already fallen."

"We've just met," I replied, trying to sound practical, trying to ignore the thrill of excitement that swept through me at his words. "You don't know anything about me."

He bent his head and nuzzled my neck. His teeth nibbled gently on my earlobe, and I gasped as unfamiliar sensations flooded through me. He massaged my back with a slow, sensuous rhythm, and my insides melted into a quivering mass of sensation and emotion. My thoughts spun like a cyclone inside my head, but instinct screamed a million warnings.

"It's all right," he soothed as I struggled to pull away. "Don't be afraid. It's only me."

I opened my mouth to reply, wanted to deny what he'd said, but it was true. I *was* afraid. Not that Michael Singleton might harm me, but of the way he made me feel.

* ~ * ~ *

A short while later, we reached our destination. The dilapidated structure was wedged firmly inside a square of sturdy tree trunks—the only thing saving it from collapsing, apparently. The roof had been devoured by leaves and low-hanging branches, while vines draped the door like skeletal fingers. Calling it a shack would have been a slight exaggeration, for it had a ways to improve before aspiring to such a lofty designation.

Michael put his hand on the rusted door latch, and gazed solemnly down at me. "This cabin is, believe it or not, the only thing that's truly mine. I guess you could call it my legacy to future generations."

I raised an eyebrow. "You've got to be joking."

His broad shoulders stiffened beneath the black wool cloak. "You mean you don't like it? You wound me, love."

The dimple winking in his cheek made me think he might be teasing me. I smiled, deciding to play along. "What's not to like? I'm sure it's one of those cabins that seems larger on the inside."

Returning the smile, he motioned me through the doorway. Moonlight illuminated his face, briefly, and I thought I saw...

Forget it, I told myself, quickly dismissing the possibility. *It's nothing. Just a trick of the moonlight.*

Michael ducked inside. The lintel brushed the top of his head, but the ceiling inside was higher than I'd expected. Michael lit a match and held the flame to a sturdy candle. Pungent sulfur singed my nostrils. My eyes gradually adjusted to the meager light, and I turned in a slow circle, taking in my surroundings.

Though only one room, the cabin did appear larger on the inside. There were two small windows on either side of the door, but they were so dirty it was impossible to see through them. Mounds of blankets and pillows dotted the floor. In the far right corner, opposite the door, was a crumbling stone fireplace covered in layers of dust and ashes. Not exactly what I'd call a legacy to be proud of.

"I built this place myself when I was twelve years old," he said, a wistful fondness softening the ragged edges of his voice.

"Twelve?" I echoed. "Well, in that case... I guess it's not bad."

"I worked on it for months. It was like an obsession. I rarely slept, and thought of little else until it was finished. My aunt began to worry something was wrong with me, because I spent every spare minute out here, alone." Seemingly lost in the memory, his gaze roamed the cabin. "It was worth it, though. I admit it isn't much to look at, but building this place taught me a lot about myself. It was my first real attempt at ascending to the Bal—"

He cleared his throat, looked away.

"I mean, I was trying to teach myself to focus on something outside myself," he finished, awkwardly.

I gauged his expression through shifting shadows. Usually, only those who wished to become priests attempted to ascend to the Balance. Magic spells could be cast by anyone, but Guardians generally possessed more power than average. Being able to first detect, then ascend to the Balance was a skill that took years of practice, and was one of the tests of initiation an acolyte was required to pass in order to join the Sacred Order.

"Did it work?" I asked.

"In a way. I'm just amazed the place is still standing. You'll be relieved to know that my skills have improved since then."

Were we talking about building skills, or magical prowess? Was Michael a Guardian, I wondered? Or had he, like Donnall, studied for years to become one, only to fail the final test of initiation?

I was about to ask at least one of those questions, when he smiled at me again. My heart lurched into my throat, and the air in the cabin grew noticeably warmer. The walls seemed to close in on me, as though the cabin were shrinking, cutting off my air.

My gaze flew to the door, as I realized, in dawning horror, how far I was from the safety of the castle.

"Your shield masked it well enough. Thank you again, by the way. I'd been counting on the wine to help me keep it under control during the feast. Only thing is... It seems to be wearing off a bit now..."

His confession faded into the nighttime cacophony of the forest. It was a moment or two before his meaning penetrated the lingering fog in my brain. When it finally did, I gasped in surprise.

"Are you saying you're...?"

His dark eyes glittered through the grainy moonlight. Our gazes met, and the breath caught in my throat.

He shrugged, nodded once, looked away.

Fear grabbed hold of my chest, and squeezed. The deafening chorus of insects was eclipsed by a sudden, loud roaring in my ears. Playing mind games in the safety of the castle was one thing. Being alone in the woods with a male who had the curse, was something else altogether

"This was a mistake," I stammered, inching toward the door. "I shouldn't have come—"

His hand snaked out and grabbed my wrist. His nostrils flared, like an animal scenting prey. "I can control it, Alena. Don't be afraid."

He had smiled like that on purpose, I realized. He wanted me to see it. But *why?* Was he deliberately trying to frighten me? Candlelight danced with the shadows on his face. I felt curiously lightheaded, had to remind myself to breathe. Deep. Even. Steady breaths.

Without warning, he released me. I stumbled backwards, rubbing my abused wrist with my other hand, thinking that if Mother were here, she'd likely admonish me with a phrase from her collection of quotes. Something like *Curiosity killed the cat*, or *Caution is the parent of safety.*

Like a child newly wakened from a deep sleep, Michael's eyes clouded over with confusion. Slowly, he walked to the opposite corner of the room. He sank into a pile of blankets, propped an elbow on one knee, and dropped his forehead in his hands.

"Illchangesmeinto," he murmured. "Sweet delight, endless night. Not *now.*" Deep breath. *"Illchangesmeinto."*

His deep, rasping voice crawled over my skin. I wrapped my arms around my waist, and hugged myself tightly. My teeth began to chatter, and wouldn't stop. The chanting ended abruptly. Michael lifted his head.

"Don't worry, love." He sounded weary, resigned. "It's only me."

Only.

"Don't tell me how to feel!" I snapped, my voice riding the edge of hysteria. "Why did you bring me here? You should have warned me about this!"

A flicker, like lightning, flashed in his eyes. "Then go," he snarled. "I can't stand the smell of your fear."

I froze. His desperate words played over and over in my mind.

The smell of my...

Fear?

The hairs on the nape of my neck prickled.

Do not suffer a cursed man to live, was the first tenet of Corvus's Sacred Law. To go against the god's commands, was to risk His wrath, and the wrath of Corvus was not to be taken lightly. But before I had a chance to consider the consequences, I crossed the room, knelt by Michael, and reached for his hand. He jerked away, as though my touch had burned him. Beads of sweat glistened on his forehead and upper lip. A gut-wrenching cry was torn from his throat, fading to a steady, low moaning, like an animal in pain.

"Michael," I said, gently. "Let me help you."

"Can't," he managed through gritted teeth. "It'll pass on its own. Just have to... wait."

His harsh breathing echoed in my ears. His throat worked as he swallowed convulsively. His skin was hot to the touch, and slick with perspiration. Violent tremors shook his body as I pried his fingers from the coarse, wool blanket.

Everything warped into unreality, like a lucid dream. I had no way to measure how long it went on, but after what seemed an eternity, his breathing calmed. He lifted his head, and peered at me through half-closed eyelids.

"Is it over?" I asked.

He nodded weakly, disentangled his hands from mine, and attempted to sit up. Failing that, he half-sat, half-leaned against the wall. His head lolled drunkenly from side to side. He looked drained of energy, and oddly vulnerable for such a large man. I smoothed the damp, tangled waves of hair from his forehead. His tongue snaked out, and scraped over his dry, cracked lips.

"Sorry, Alena. Didn't mean to—"

"Parvi refert," I answered automatically. The literal translation was, *It matters little,* but it had been

no small thing for me to kneel there helplessly and watch him suffer. "How often does this happen?"

"It's not... I don't know," he began haltingly. "It doesn't really follow any kind of pattern. More often, I think, when the moon is full."

The next full moon was weeks away. *So what had triggered this episode?* I wondered. I waited for him to continue, but he pressed his lips firmly together, and turned his face into the shadows. A million questions swirled through my brain, but I realized that Michael was in no condition to answer them now.

Exhausted, I burrowed into the pile of blankets and rested my chin on my knees. I closed my eyes, let my thoughts break up and drift away, and lost myself to the music of crickets and locusts in fragile harmony.

When I was a little girl, I hated to go to sleep. I was in love with the night, the way everything looked different when viewed by moonlight. I thought I could actually see the air shimmering with magic, and wanted to absorb every wondrous moment of it. Father was a night owl too, but Mother liked to fall asleep at dusk and wake with the dawn. Bestiae *will get you,* she used to say. *He's got a taste for little girls who go outside after dark.*

Michael's hand on my shoulder jerked me back to the present.

"Alena, wake up. It's nearly dawn."

Every muscle in my body felt stiff and sore. I rubbed my eyes and stifled a groan. The sound of Michael's boots against the splintered floorboards merged with the steady beat of rain dripping through cracks in the roof. I inhaled deeply, tasted mold and damp wool on the back of my tongue, then rolled over and buried my face in my cocoon of blankets. A droplet of cold rain splashed on my nose.

"Alena."

"Hmm?"

"We should get back to the gathering, before someone comes looking for us."

Wood creaked and groaned as he sat down next to me. Blankets slid back and forth as he shifted position. The fog of sleep dissipated slowly, as it always did, remnants of incoherent dreams trailing in its wake. I moistened my lips, hating the sour, gummy taste of waking up, longing for my toothbrush and little tin of cleansing powder. My eyes slid open, but it was a moment or two before the world swam into focus.

Michael leaned against the wall, one arm resting on his drawn—up knee. Memories of last night flooded back to me, and I tried to silence the alarm bells ringing in my head. As the only child of the Guardian of the Dead, I was training to follow in my father's footsteps. The fact that I had not yet passed the final exam, did not quite render my education useless. I knew what I was dealing with. After last night, it was all too obvious that he suffered from the disease peculiar to our people.

Michael was cursed.

An abomination.

Knowing that, still I chose to stay with him. After seeing him struggle with the sickness, still I chose to remain by his side. I couldn't blame my stupidity on his good looks alone. So, when my father asked me where I'd been all night—which he was sure to do, the minute I arrived home—what on earth was I going to say?

I knew I ought to be repulsed by what Michael was, not fascinated and intrigued, but all I could think about was how good it felt to lay cuddled in our nest of blankets while the forest stirred to life around us. I shifted closer to Michael's big, warm body, and tentatively rested my head on his shoulder. His arm slid around me, gently cupping my waist.

But, as Robert Frost observed, nothing gold can stay. All too soon, my mind resumed its incessant stream of annoying chatter. Michael seemed blithely unaware of the danger he was in. A result, I surmised, of too many years spent living in the land of the *advena.* A shield was hard to sustain for long periods of time. It would prevent a Guardian from performing *captare,* but a simple shield would not completely mask Michael's illness—especially not if someone else witnessed an episode like the one I witnessed last night.

That realization instantly banished the fantasy I had awoken to and sent me plunging, kicking and screaming, back into the icy waters of reality. I rolled over and sat up, blowing errant strands of hair from my eyes.

"A shield won't hide it forever, Michael."

His big body tensed beside me. "Don't worry. I have it under control."

"Take it from me: Donnall isn't the type to let things go. His father, Innes, is the Captain of the Guard. It won't take much for Donnall to convince him to arrest you."

At the mention of my half-brother, Michael let out a rumbling growl, soft and low. His eyes glittered.

Tiny pinpricks of light flickered through the grainy shadows.

"The land of the *advena* has its own dangers, Alena. What makes you think I'd be safe there?"

"Why wouldn't you be?" I asked, confused by what seemed to be a lack of concern for his own safety. "The Guard can't arrest you, if you aren't here."

His eyebrows raised in silent disagreement.

"Do you think the guards will follow you?" I asked. "Why would they do that?"

He shrugged. "It happens. And if I leave, I'll never find—" He stopped, took a deep breath, looked away.

"Never find what?"

Minutes passed in stony silence. A muscle jumped in his jaw, and he shook his head. "Forget it," he mumbled. "Doesn't matter." He jumped to his feet, and extended a hand to help me up. "Come on, let's get out of here. I'm hungry."

I hesitated a moment, then placed my smaller hand in his, leaving warmth and contentment in the puddle of blankets on the floor.

Michael tossed me his cloak. "Here. Put this on."

He strode briskly to the door, yanked it open, and disappeared through the misty rain. I muttered a curse, and hurried after him, spotted his dark, wavy hair and broad shoulders poking above a thick clump of weeds. He motioned for me to follow. Mud sucked at my boots as I fought my way through the prickly underbrush.

The sky had lightened by the time we reached the river, but the sun remained hidden behind a sheet of thick gray clouds. I was grateful for the hooded cloak, for it kept the rain from soaking through to my clothing. Moles and chipmunks scurried through the underbrush. The patter of rain on the leaves echoed in my ears.

It would take over an hour to reach the castle. Once there, Michael and I would go our separate ways, and there was a good chance this was the last time we would ever be alone together. I couldn't bear to think about the danger that might be waiting for him when he returned, so I tried to ignore it. Michael didn't seem concerned about it, I told myself, so why should I be? Maybe I *was* overreacting. Maybe his situation wasn't as dire as I was making it out to be. Maybe he would pass the Evaluation, and the Sacred Order would have to let him go.

I found myself unable to suppress my growing curiosity about who he was and what he was doing here. The question slipped from my lips before I could stop it.

"Michael, why did you come back to Blackwater Hills?"

He stopped walking, and turned to face me. "I have my reasons."

"Which are?" I asked, when it became obvious he wasn't going to elaborate.

"Sorry, Alena. I can't explain it. Not to you."

Logically, I knew he had no reason to trust me. Even so, the words were like a slap in the face. I stepped in front of him, and tried to read his expression through a jungle of wet black waves.

"Michael," I began, desperate to make him understand. "Listen to me very carefully. Sacred Law teaches us that males who are cursed are an abomination. To suffer you to live, is to risk the wrath of Corvus. If you stay, sooner or later, someone is going to notice. You'll be arrested, chained in the basement of the castle, and the Guardians will test you mercilessly before bringing you to trial.

"When they find you guilty, they will burn you alive in a ceremonial bonfire with no spells to protect you from Venefica's *daemons.* Your soul will not be allowed to enter the Otherworld, and will wander for eternity, lost in the void of the Shadowlands."

He nodded, wearily. "My father was a priest. Don't you think I know that?"

Exasperated, I threw up my hands. "Then why stay here, Michael? If you leave now, none of it will happen!"

His jaw clenched. "I can't leave," he muttered. "There's no other way in."

In his voice was something I couldn't quite place, a tone that reached in and touched the core of my emotions. I saw fear in his eyes—a flash, like lightning, then gone with a flicker of his thick, black lashes. I was overcome by an urgent desire to protect him. A ridiculous desire, for never had I seen a man more capable of taking care of himself than Michael Singleton.

"I'm not a Guardian—*yet,"* I confessed. "I can't defend you."

He grimaced. "What makes you think I would even *want* you to defend me?"

"You don't have a choice, you know," I retorted, stung by the rejection. "The Sacred Order will appoint a Guardian for you, and when you fail the evaluation, he will have no choice but to sentence you to death."

"Certain of my failure, are you? Why do you care so much, anyway?"

The rhythm of raindrops picked up speed. Branches creaked and groaned as the wind tossed them one way and another. The forest sighed in halfhearted protest. Birds and wildlife scattered, searching for shelter from the imminent deluge. A blush warmed my cheeks as his gaze searched mine, and I felt it again—the urge to shield him from danger, keep him safe, no matter the cost.

"I'd offer the same advice to anyone," I answered, finally. It was a weak denial of my emotions—not to mention, unconvincing. A slow smile spread across his face.

"Liar."

His rough whisper sent chills down my spine. The smile grew, as my cheeks burned hotter. A thousand questions crowded on the tip of my tongue, but shock had stolen my voice. Gradually, the hideous expression faded, and a resigned look settled over his face.

"Do you really believe that death is something I fear?" he asked in a raw voice, as though he was fighting to get the words out. "It's not, you know. For someone like me, staying alive is probably worse."

CHAPTER THREE
Those Who Worry

Alena Andrick
Blackwater Hills

I plodded up the grassy hillside, only partially aware of the bright rays of sunlight slicing through the clouds. The heavy rain had slowed to occasional drizzle, and the winds had calmed, leaving the air feeling balmy. Everything felt different, somehow. *I* felt different. Before meeting Michael, I had been a whole person: *Alena Andrick, nineteen years old, a solitary being.* Now I felt disconnected from myself and my surroundings, half the person I had been before yesterday.

But maybe the reality was that I'd always been half; I just never realized it until Michael kissed me.

Even the castle I was born in looked eerily unfamiliar, smaller somehow, less imposing. A few of the rectangular windows were cracked or broken. Sections of stone were nicked or crumbling. Weeds had taken over the flower garden, sprouting between cracks in the path leading to the front door. Smoke from the dying bonfire drifted through the air. As was always the case the morning after a gathering, those who had overindulged in ceremonial wine were passed out here and there. Bodies littered the meadow like the aftermath of battle.

I crossed the narrow, stone bridge and stopped just inside the archway, staring up at the carving above the door:

The word *Reviresco* had been chiseled beneath the cryptic symbol. In the tongue of the ancients, it meant *I Flourish Again,* and was the motto of clan Maxwell. The man who had built the castle, James Douglas Maxwell, had been a bastard son of Robert Maxwell, second earl of Nithsdale. James fled Scotland in the seventeenth century, and eventually settled in Blackwater Hills. Other descendants of Corvus soon followed. Maxwells, Singletons, Andricks, Campbells, Kendricks, and MacDonalds merged with the native Acadians to create a haven for themselves and their children. A place where they could be free to worship Corvus, far from the persecution of intolerant, superstitious humans.

Our world was wilderness, untamed forest as far as the eye could see. A ring of white-capped mountains rose through lush, colorful foliage in the fall and spring, stood guard during the little death of winter, and reflected the glory of Soluna in the heat of summer. The air was clean, the taste of the river sweet and pure. Game was plentiful, the ground fertile, vegetation abundant. We wanted for nothing.

The world beyond the Great Shield was much different. Highways and concrete that suffocated the earth. Overcrowded cities teeming with disease and pollution. Children begging for food in the streets. Crime and punishment, poisoned water, dissension, and war. Sometimes I wasn't sure I believed it all, though. Books from the land of the *advena* were full of contradictions. Some truth may have been woven through the fabric of fiction, but it was impossible to separate fantasy from outright lies. Nevertheless, life seemed to be nothing but chaos, beyond the Shield. Blackwater Hills may have been boring at times, but at least it was safe and predictable.

Or at least it had been, up until last night.

I pushed open the heavy, plank door and stepped inside the entry hall. The creak of rusted hinges sounded unusually loud. Directly across the foyer, was the wide stone staircase, curving like the tail of a dragon to the second floor. Upstairs were two unoccupied guest rooms which shared a bath closet and privy, a private meeting room for the priests of the Sacred Order, Father's chamber, and Grandfather Allistair's room. To the left of the staircase, was the door to the north tower and the alcove that lead into the Great Hall. To the right, was the door to the south tower, and the alcove that led into the kitchen.

I sighed in relief to find no stragglers from last night roaming the entry hall. The last thing I wanted to do was stop and make small—talk. As I crossed the room, my soft—soled leather boots made the barest whisper of sound on the smooth stone. I couldn't rid my mind of the frightening image of Michael's smile, couldn't help thinking that, ordinarily, he went to great lengths to hide the deformity — especially from humans. The fact that he revealed it to me could have been no accident. He was trying to tell me something, I thought. But what?

As I tried to guess Michael's reasons, fragments of memory teased my mind: *A little girl with long, red-gold hair kneels in the dust, stares down at something in rapt fascination. Magic hums through her fingertips as she caresses the smooth, dry surface, and she feels the first strong stirrings of a power she will eventually work hard to develop. Fear mingles with excitement—a connection the Otherworld!*

Understanding flooded through me, suddenly, and I knew right where to begin searching for the answer. I slipped through the door to the north tower, and climbed the winding staircase to my chamber. There were no windows in the narrow passage, and the tiny arrow-slits cut into the stone had long since been sealed against the cold. I felt my way along, counting each step until I reached the octagonal landing.

As I lifted the latch and pushed open the door, I began a mental list of everything I would need. First and foremost, was the lantern I kept on the bedside table. Next, I needed to find a backpack and a waterskin. It was half a day's walk to Elise's cabin, so I had to remember to bring along some food—

"Where have you been?"

My heart skipped a beat, and I stopped in my tracks. Squinting through the gloom, I noticed the slight figure standing across the room, in the shadows of the fireplace. My throat dried up, and I swallowed reflexively.

"Father? What a nice... surprise."

Fine-boned and short of stature, with a mass of reddish-gray hair trailing over his shoulders, my father did not *look* intimidating. But what he lacked in height, he made up for with his formidable presence. There was no distinction between Claudius Andrick, Guardian of the Dead and Claudius Andrick, sire of Alena. Both had an aura that commanded respect and attention, not to mention an uncanny talent for detecting even the most elaborate of fabrications.

He was dressed, as always, in the long, brown robe which identified him as a priest and member of the Sacred Order. The coarse material was belted at his waist with a knotted piece of string, but the hem was too long. It puddled around his ankles, spilling over the tips of his boots. As he moved towards me, he looked to be gliding above the smooth stone floor.

He stopped mere inches from my face and made a harsh sound, like a cross between a cough and a growl. I told myself he was simply clearing his throat, and blamed the sudden flare of light in his eyes on the waning fire in the hearth, for my father very rarely let his temper get the best of him.

"Did you mate with him, Alena?" His tone was deceptively soft. Like a velvet blanket, it settled over my skin.

"No!" I said quickly, averting my eyes.

He chanted something in the tongue of the ancients. I struggled to translate the words, and could not. My father's lilting, musical accent had always reminded me of water trickling over a rocky hillside. But now there flowed through it a harsh undercurrent, as mighty as the raging Blackwater River. The sound vibrated though my skull. Tingling numbness spread through my limbs.

His hand slid from the sleeve of his robe. He grabbed my wrist, and squeezed so hard the bones shifted. I wanted to cry out from the pain, but my body felt frozen, weightless and heavy at the same time. His skin glowed with a faint, greenish light, and his dark eyes glittered with hundreds of tiny, whirling stars. They flickered, broke apart, swirled back together. Time slowed, then ceased to have any meaning.

"You know the punishment for disobeying Sacred Law, so heed this warning, daughter, for it is the only one I will give you. Stay far away from the abomination. Resist the spell that he has put you under. Do not speak his name. Do not conjure him with your mind. The Law of Corvus is truth. The truth is sacred."

With a motion that sent me sprawling halfway across the room, he let go of my wrist, and I doubled over, gasping for air. Fear formed a churning knot in the pit of my stomach. My legs trembled violently, then gave out altogether. I slumped into an ungainly heap against the side of the bed. My chest heaved with the effort to draw in breath.

The sharp *clip-clip-clip* of my father's retreating footsteps sounded unusually loud. I raised my head and looked over my shoulder.

How dare you treat me like a child! I wanted to scream, but all I that emerged was a moan of frustration. The hem of my father's brown robe swirled about his ankles as he spun on his heels and stalked from the room, slamming the heavy door behind him.

* ～ * ～ *

Abnormalities such as sharper than normal canines, claw-like fingernails, and excessive body hair were common among those who suffer from the curse. However, a male could display no such characteristics, and still be found guilty. I had to admit, though, I had never seen nor heard of anyone—be they cursed, or not—displaying anything like what Michael had shown me last night.

I couldn't explain why, but I had a strong gut feeling that there was a passage in Sacred Law that would explain Michael's deformity. That passage, coupled with the evidence I intended to unearth from the basement, might be enough to persuade the Sacred Order to let Michael live.

The Sacred Law of Corvus was a collection of scrolls stored in the library on the first floor of the castle. Most of the scrolls had been written during the uprising, almost two centuries ago, when the Sacred Order had been established to overthrow the Tyrannical Merula. The library was the private domain of the Guardian of the Dead, and it was with his permission only that priests of the Sacred Order were granted access. For the rest of the tribe, the library was strictly off-limits, and it was considered an egregious sin for a lay person to set eyes upon the scrolls of Sacred Law. Even as an acolyte, I was forbidden to read them.

I couldn't risk getting caught in my father's library, but I still believed he had no right to expect me to obey his dictates. I was nineteen years old, a child no longer. Most girls my age had lifemates, children of their own, and were no longer subject to their parents' authority. Besides, *Do not conjure him with your mind* seemed like an odd way of saying, *Do not think of Michael.* So, naturally, I couldn't keep from doing it. His likeness took shape in my mind's eye: tall, and strong, with that powerful, devastating beauty only a man could possess. He'd make handsome sons. With hair as black as midnight, smooth, tanned skin, and those impossibly dark eyes.

I tried to ignore the nervous tingling in my gut that felt suspiciously like instinct warning me to be careful. But the urge to protect Michael overpowered my instinct for self-preservation.

Don't think about why. Just do it. Figure out why you did it, later.

My plan was to pack food and water for my journey along the river to Elise's cabin. After that, I was going to sneak down into the castle basement and search the tomb for evidence. With the evidence in hand, I was going to enlist the help of Elise's *lifemate,* Tarren Campbell. As a priest, Tarren's word held more weight than mine, and if Tarren agreed to act as Michael's Guardian, Michael might actually have a chance of getting out of Blackwater Hills alive.

I grabbed my backpack and headed downstairs, passed through the arched stone corridor, and entered the kitchen. Immediately, I was overcome by the sharp smell of bread dough rising in the oven. A fire roared in the open firepit. The blackened cast iron pot hung above the flames, bubbling merrily. Sayla Kendrick was pushing a broom in the corner. Shaina, Donnall's *lifemate*, was perched atop a stool beside the long, plank table in the center of the room. My mother stood on the opposite side of the kitchen, one hand braced on the iron washtub, the other planted firmly on her ample waist.

When she saw me, her eyes narrowed beneath a fringe of black bangs. I cleared my throat and tried to look innocent, but my cheeks warmed beneath my mother's penetrating stare.

"What are you doing here?" I blurted out, before she had a chance to wonder what I was up to.

Mother forced a smile that didn't quite reach her eyes. "Just redding up. Everything was such a mess, and Claudius asked us to help, since you were nowhere around. Now that you're here, can you give us a hand?"

"Actually, I was just on my way out. I'm going to stay with Elise for a few days."

I thought I saw relief in her expression. My scalp prickled in warning.

"Oh," she said, as she helped Shaina sort through the mounds of leftover chicken on the counter. "That's probably for the best, then. Considering."

My mother's *lifemate,* Innes was the Captain of the Guard. She would, naturally, be among the first to learn the news. A flurry of moths took up residence in my stomach, and beat at my insides with fluttering wings. My palms started sweating, and I resisted the urge to wipe them on the legs of my trousers.

"Considering what?"

I already knew. I just wanted her say it. Mother's lips tightened in a grim line. Using the tip of a knife, she pushed the scraps of chicken into a lopsided pile.

Sayla leaned the broom against the wall, and crossed both arms beneath her modest breasts. Eyebrows raised, she gave me a quick once-over. Then she pursed her lips, and looked disapproving. "Michael Singleton has been arrested on suspicion, and the Sacred Order has pronounced him *Maledictus*—pending an evaluation, of course. They're holding him in Jackson's cabin for the time being, while Innes gathers the Guard for escort. He'll be kept here, in the dungeon. Didn't Claudius tell you?"

Even though I'd been expecting them, the words were like a punch in the gut. My heart hammered against my chest, and I heard a roaring in my ears, like rushing water. I leaned against the wall as all the strength drained out of my legs.

Shaina's eyes widened. She slid off the stool, and rushed to my side. "Alena! Do you feel okay?"

I took a deep breath, and nodded shakily. "I felt dizzy... for a second. I'm okay now."

Shaina looked unconvinced. Mother wiped her hands on her apron, and bustled over to assist me. She took hold of my arm, and led me to the wooden bench that stretched beneath a row of rectangular windows on the south wall of the kitchen.

"Sit down," she ordered. "I'll make some tea."

"No, I don't want—" I began, but she waved away the protest.

"You look awfully pale. Have you eaten today?"

"Not yet," I confessed, and my mother sighed. She crossed the room to the stove, returning a few minutes later with a steaming mug of blackberry tea cradled in her work—roughed hands.

"The stew should be another hour or so," she said, handing me the mug. "But there's a loaf of fresh bread to tide you over."

I sipped at the tea, and shook my head. "I'm all right," I insisted. "Really."

Mother frowned. "You are *not* all right, Alena. You need to eat. Give us this day, our daily bread. Your body is your temple; you must honor and nourish it."

I scowled. "Fine. I'll eat some bread. But I really should get going. I'm burning daylight."

Anxious to be on my way, I watched as Mother ambled over to the sideboard, picked up a knife, and began slicing the bread. Her movements were precise and economical, smooth with the ease of long practice. She topped two slices with big blobs of softened butter, then placed them on a towel and handed them to me. I set the mug of tea on the bench, accepting her offering with a nod of thanks.

I bit through the thick crust and sank my teeth into the warm, spongy center. Sweet melted butter slid over my tongue, while crumbs rained down the front of my shirt. I wiped my mouth with the towel, swallowed what remained of the tea, and then looked up to find all three women staring worriedly down at me.

I met each of their gazes in turn, but was unable to hold them for very long, afraid that all my secrets would be revealed through my eyes, and they would be able to see how desperate I was to go to Michael. Mother would want an explanation, but I had no idea why I felt such strong feelings for a man I'd known only a couple of days. It made no sense, and part of me was afraid to examine the situation too closely.

A few moments later, I heard Mother sigh, then watched out of the corner of my eye as she crossed the room to check on the stew. The crackle and hiss of the fire seemed to bounce off the thick stone walls. The bubbles boiling and bursting in the pot sounded like sharp hooves striking a rocky mountainside. Discordant chirping filtered through the brittle window glass, underscored by the plaintive cry of the wind.

I stared at Mother's back as she stirred the contents of the pot with a long-handled spoon. A chunk of her short hair had worked its way below her collar, breaking the even line of silky black on the back of her neck. Rounded shoulders and wide hips were interrupted by the faintest suggestion of a waist. Her sturdy legs, booted feet set slightly apart, were camouflaged beneath a black wool skirt.

She lifted the spoon from the pot and hung it on a hook above the fireplace. "I noticed you talking to Michael during the feast," she began.

My cheeks warmed. Perspiration prickled under my arms. I stared at the spoon she had used to stir the stew. Drops of liquid collected on its tip, broke free, and splattered on the floor.

"I know you spent the night with him, Alena. I can't say as I blame you," she quickly added, holding up a hand to ward off any protest. "He's a beautiful man, the very image of his father. When Sayla and I were about your age, all the girls were crazy in love with Branden Singleton."

Sayla sighed wistfully. "Remember how hard Jenna Alexander cried when he chose Erin Campbell for his *lifemate?*" She asked Mother, and the expression on her face made me wonder if she might have shed a few tears herself.

Mother smiled and nodded her head, but an air of sadness seemed to settle over her. "Branden was a priest who took his duties very seriously," she explained. "His loyalty to Corvus came before everything. When Erin died birthing Michael, something inside Branden died, as well. He was different after that, no more the soft-spoken, studious Guardian we had come to love and respect. He became aggressive, belligerent, and even violent at times. It wasn't that he didn't love his son. I mean, I'm sure he did..."

She let the sentence trail away, picked up a washrag, and began methodically cleaning the surface of the counter. "Every parent knows that a child's physical and emotional well-being ought to come before his own. A father has an obligation to nurture the spirit he's called into the physical world. Not doing so upsets the Balance, and the price for that is always high. Everyone suffers, not only he and the child. As a priest, surely Branden knew this, but it was as though simply being around Michael brought out the worst in him."

"Well, Cora, you must admit that Branden wasn't the first male to upset the Balance," Sayla interjected. "And he won't be the last, unfortunately. I know nurturing is traditionally left to females, but now I'm wondering if Branden might have been able to sense the curse in his son. Maybe his reaction was instinct, something he had no control over."

Mother brushed the bangs from her eyes, and sighed heavily. "All I know is, it was painful to watch. Stella, may Corvus guide her spirit, did the best she could. But she was barely more than a child herself."

Did Michael's father beat him, I wondered? Or did he use words as his weapons, instead?

I wanted to ask, but at the same time, wasn't sure I really wanted to know. Sayla had been right when she'd said, it was an all too common situation. The tribe accepted it the same way we accepted that sometimes the insects ravaged our crops, that winter was often fatally harsh, and that death would be the inevitable end to our journey through the physical world. No one wanted to acknowledge the cruel way some males treated their children. It was painful to watch, but since nothing could be done about it, we mostly chose not to watch.

I let my long hair fall forward to hide my expression, and stared down at my hands clasped together in my lap. I wasn't sure what the history of Michael's relationship with his father had to do with now—with the fact that Michael had just been arrested by the Order his father had once served so diligently. That Mother had broached the topic at all, indicated she suspected there was something between Michael and me. She would never forbid me to see him, as my father had, but maybe the story was her way of warning me to proceed with caution.

"But that was a long time ago," she resumed, dismissing the past with a shake of her head. "I'd be the last person to know how these things have affected Michael, if they even have. He may have had a good life out there in the land of the *advena,* but he's lived amongst humans almost as long as he's lived amongst the tribe. None of us knows the man Michael Singleton has grown up to be."

Shaina sat demurely on her stool, offering no opinion, but looking suitably attentive. Her *lifemate* was, after all, a member of the Guard, so it was no great mystery whose side she was on. Sayla shook her head, and with a *tsk* of her tongue, bent over to tend the fire. Sparks flew upward on a cloud of smoke as she dropped a few logs atop the pile of glowing embers.

One thing Cora Maxwell always freely offered was good advice, and I knew I ought to seriously consider heeding it. Trouble was, I couldn't get my emotions in accord with the logic of my brain. I didn't know how to turn off the insistent longing, the desperate need I felt to be with Michael. It was as though my soul was in turmoil, and would remain so as long as we were separated. The sense of urgency was disturbing. All I could think about was Michael. Nothing else seemed important.

I was afraid to tell my mother how I felt, afraid she would react the same way my father had reacted. I didn't want her to think, as he did, that Michael had cast some sort of spell over me. I didn't want to be like everyone else and assume the worst, didn't want to fall into the trap of doubting my own instincts, because I could feel it down to the marrow of my bones.

Cursed or not, Michael did not deserve to be executed.

And, Corvus help me, I was about to risk everything to prove it.

* ~ * ~ *

Unable to talk my way out of helping in the kitchen, it was nearly an hour later when, backpack and lantern in hand, I crept down the stairs to the castle basement. Occasionally inhabited by wandering spirits, the basement consisted of three cavernous sections. Each section had been designed for a specific use. On the left, was the Sanctuary. To the right, was the Tomb. Directly ahead, through a heavily bolted steel door, was the castle dungeon. At the bottom of the stairs, I veered right, strode through the narrow passageway, and entered the sacred burial chamber.

I held my lantern high, and looked around. Shadows climbed the rough stone walls—flickering in annoyance, as though my presence disturbed them. In darkened corners, secrets slumbered beneath layers of centuries' old dust, for those who might have sought to uncover them were dust, themselves. Beneath the tomb, accessed through a trapdoor in the center of the floor, was one of four spirit communication chambers located in the area protected by the Great Shield. In the upper chamber, crammed together on every available surface, languished the skulls of every man, woman, and child who had died while in Blackwater Hills. Even the *advena* were buried here. Only the skulls of cursed males were not allowed. The cursed were forbidden to receive the Ritual of Silence, for their souls were not permitted entrance to the Otherworld.

But it was here. I saw it. More than one, in fact.

I figured that the evidence I needed must be on one of the shelves closest to the floor, for I was younger then, and wouldn't have been able to reach very high. If I began my search in the far right corner nearest the door, then worked my way around the room, I figured I was bound to come across one eventually.

By the time I found one on the bottom shelf, buried way in the back, I was coated in a fine layer of dust, and my knees ached from squatting on the damp stone floor. I sat back on my heels and examined the skull, turning it this way and that in my hands. It was unremarkable, except for its teeth, which appeared larger than normal with curved, elongated canines protruding from both the upper and lower jaws. I ran my tongue along the inside of my mouth, to compare. The molars looked to be wider and flatter, as well. I counted thirty-six teeth altogether.

Four more than should have been there.

I set the skull on the floor by the lantern, and began to search for others with same deformity. I found seven more on that shelf alone. The shelf above it held three, the next eight, then eleven. I took them out, and lined them up in a row.

"What are these skulls doing buried in the consecrated tomb?" I whispered.

Sixty empty eye sockets stared back at me, mute and indifferent to my curiosity. I began to replace the skulls on the shelves where I'd found them. All except one, which I hid inside my backpack. I fastened the buttons at the top, then slung the long strap of the backpack over my shoulder. The unfamiliar weight bumped against my waist as I strode briskly toward the exit, and it occurred to me that the skull's owner might object to its removal from the sacred resting place. I stopped for a moment, closed my eyes, and offered up a silent prayer to his spirit—thanking him for his generosity, and promising to return his skull as soon as possible.

Just as I reached the doorway, I heard a loud *clank!* followed by what sounded like a group of men arguing and shouting about something. The words weren't clear, just an urgent cacophony of voices that echoed and bounced off the thick stone walls. The noises seemed to be coming from the staircase—the only way in or out of the castle basement.

Corvus help me. The last thing I wanted to do was get caught down here by a member of the Guard. The Sacred Order took serious issue with anyone who attempted to interfere with an Evaluation, and I didn't want to be in the position of having to defend my actions. Not, at least, until I had irrefutable evidence to back up what the priests would surely view as an heretical theory.

I eyed the trapdoor in the center of the floor, wondering if I had the courage to hide beneath it. I decided I didn't, and backed up, to the farthest corner of the tomb. Then I reached down and extinguished the lantern. My heart pounded against my ribs, and I bit my lip so hard I tasted blood. The ruckus grew louder, seemed to be drawing closer, and it suddenly dawned on me what was happening: Innes had mustered up his escort, and the guards were trying to get Michael inside the dungeon.

By the sound of it, Michael was not cooperating.

CHAPTER FOUR
Michael Speaks

Michael Singleton
Blackwater Hills

"Does he have a Guardian yet, do you think?

"How the fuck should I know? They don't tell us lowlife *stultissimi* nothin'."

Donnall grinned. "'Idiots,' huh? That's what we are?"

Seamus shrugged. "It's what the priests think of us, leastways. You know how they are, Donnall. Heads up their asses, the lot of 'em."

Donnall grunted agreement. "Give him wine, then," he ordered. "But not too much. I don't want him to be numb. I want him to feel it."

Michael slumped against the cage wall. Iron shackles had been locked around his wrists and ankles, and his arms had been bound to his sides by a length of chain securely wrapped around his upper torso. His sharp gaze followed the guard's every movement. As Donnall paced back and forth before the mouth of the cage, the metal keying looped around his belt jangled against his denim—clad hip. The sound, like black smoke rising from a bonfire, lingered in the air, cloying and oppressive.

His death knell.

Michael tried to control his agitated panting, slow his pounding heart, and subdue his fear. The effort proved as futile as escape was likely to be. No amount of reciting poetry or chanting a ridiculous mantra was going to tame the overwhelming urge to tear Donnall's throat out. The savage fury consumed every fiber of his being. He ached for the taste of his former rival's blood, imagined the hot elixir flowing over his teeth and tongue, warming his insides, feeding his power. A growl of warning rumbled in his throat. His mouth watered, and he nearly howled in frustration.

Donnall stopped pacing. Michael shuddered as the guard's cold, green gaze raked the length of his body.

"Keep an eye on him, Seamus. I'm going to tell the Guardian of the Dead we've arrived."

Seamus nodded at Donnall's retreating back. He strode to the opposite side of the cage, squatted down on his heels, and began rummaging through a pile of backpacks.

While the scruffy—looking guard was occupied with his search, Michael took in his surroundings. The basement of the castle was dank and cold. Moss coated the walls and floor in random splotches, like dark green paint. Though the cage was deep and roomy, there was only one way in or out. The basement's only exit was approximately thirty feet from the door of the cell, which meant he'd have to get past Seamus, up the staircase and through the castle, then deal with Donnall once he got outside.

But first things first: How to free himself from the elaborate tangle of iron?

He had to get his hands on the keying fastened to the guard's belt. As he ruminated on how to accomplish that seemingly impossible feat, Michael took a deep breath, and tried to swallow his mounting anxiety. Cold sweat bathed his skin beneath his clothing, and the smell of his own fear made his stomach roil in sickening rebellion.

Seamus ended his search, and stood up. Clutching a cask of ceremonial wine in one meaty hand and a crude, wooden goblet in the other, Donnall's partner-in-crime strolled awkwardly across the floor. As the guard came closer, Michael caught the mingled scents of peppermint and unwashed male. A violent shudder wracked him. Chains rattled and clanked as he jerked against his bonds.

Seamus's nose was long and pointed, giving him a somewhat lizard-like appearance. An unkempt beard obscured the lower portion of his face, and his reddish-brown hair was snarled and matted. Deep set brown eyes, sparkling with hostility, peered beneath the shelf of his protruding forehead.

"Quit yer squirmin'," he ordered, getting down on one knee and placing the goblet on a flat section of moss-covered rock. "It ain't gonna do no good."

Michael growled a warning, low in his throat. Seamus's bushy eyebrows lifted, and he snorted in amusement. "Don't get me wrong. I admire that you got some fight in ya, you know? Ain't no kind of man just lays down and takes what's coming to him, even if he does deserve it."

There was a loud *pop!* as Seamus's pudgy fingers pried the cork from the mouth of the cask. He poured a measure of wine into the goblet, then set the cask aside. He shook his head and stared down at the floor, a frown creasing his dirt-streaked forehead.

"Then again," he mused thoughtfully, slanting Michael a glance out of the corner of his eye. "You ain't *really* a man. Are you?"

*   ~   *   ~   *

"The perversion of His ultimate gift, In Bestiae Corpore Transmuto, *angers our great and powerful Father. To atone for our sins, we must purge the tainted blood. Males who are cursed shall be banned from the glory of His kingdom, the Otherworld. Spare the abomination, dishonor the Lord Corvus, and He will claim his due,* In Vindicare!"

Michael felt their gazes on him, heavy with judgment. Time seemed to stand still. Sweat broke out on his forehead and under his arms, and his cheeks flooded with hot color.

Their teacher, the Honorable Guardian Ivan James, relished theatrical inflections and dramatic pauses and couldn't resist sprinkling them liberally throughout every lecture. Michael tried to keep his expression blank, his eyes straight ahead, focused on nothing in particular. Thanking the gods that this was the last day of class until after the Spring Solstice celebration, he held his breath, and silently drummed his fingers on the desktop.

"What we must come to understand, is that when we sacrifice the cursed, we do not do so in vain," Ivan resumed. "May they go willingly to their fiery deaths, knowing it is for the good of the tribe and the glory of Corvus."

A large black fly landed inches from Michael's hand. His fingers stilled, and he stared at it intently, memorizing every line of its fragile wings, the way its tiny black body looked inert, yet somehow in motion, watchful for any hint of danger.

"Blessed are the children of Corvus, for those who obey His Sacred Law will be spared the everlasting torment of the Shadowlands—the domain of the wicked witch, Venefica!"

Michael cringed inside, thinking how naive he'd once been, how much he'd truly believed that there was a benevolent entity who watched over him and actually cared about what happened to him. When he'd lain in bed as a child, licking the wounds in his self-esteem, he'd imagined that Corvus was testing him much the way the Beast God had been tested by His sister, the Witch. If he passed the god's tests, Michael was certain, he would one day be rewarded and blessed by his true father; he would one day share in the glory of the Otherworld.

But as Michael grew older, signs of the god's disfavor grew more and more obvious. He knew it was only a matter of time before others began to notice them too. The events of the past several months had convinced him that Corvus had better things to worry about than saving yet another Singleton male from the void of the Shadowlands.

At least, he thought, he'd have plenty of company.

The fly, spooked by some unseen threat, took flight. Out of the corner of his eye, Michael spotted Donnall Maxwell behind the long, plank table on the opposite side of the room. Donnall was sprawled lazily upon the wooden bench, legs stretched out, chin cupped in the palm of his hand, cool green gaze fixed firmly on Michael.

"The law of Corvus contains wisdom greater than any we may seek to understand. Only by His mercy are we granted everlasting life. The law of Corvus is truth. The truth is sacred."

"The law of Corvus is truth. The truth is sacred," the class responded automatically.

Michael felt the weight of Donnall's scrutiny pressing down on him. He shifted in his seat, wishing he had the power to make himself invisible. Donnall made no secret of the fact that he aspired to join the priesthood when he came of age, seizing every opportunity to hone his skills as a Guardian in preparation for the day he'd be permitted to don his robes.

Donnall had, in the meantime, apparently decided to practice his priestly skills on the Singleton family. Hardly surprising under the circumstances, but not something Michael wanted to encourage. Michael was twelve years old. Too young to be executed, but not too young to be jailed for evaluation, if the Sacred Order suspected he might pose some danger to the tribe.

Wallowing in the mire of his own dismal musings, Michael flinched when Ivan clapped twice to signal the end of class. Head down, disheveled black hair veiling his eyes, Michael rose from the bench and shouldered his way through the throng of students crowding the doorway.

Once outside, he inhaled a deep, calming breath of the warm spring air. The afternoon sun was hot, but not oppressively so. Bright rays streamed through breaks in the lush canopy of trees overhead. Michael *tilted his head and squinted up at the sky, silently debating whether to fix the broken shutters for Aunt Stella like he'd promised, or spend the rest of the day fishing at the river. Winter was a long ways off, he decided; he had plenty of time to catch up on repairs to the cabin. Besides, fresh bass for supper would go a long way toward persuading his aunt to forgive his laziness.*

"Hey, Singleton!"

Michael's jaw clenched. He turned around, hands curling into fists at his sides. Donnall Maxwell stalked toward him, flanked by his pack —Ian and Seamus MacDonald, and that little weasel, Tarren Campbell. The look on Donnall's face dared Michael to challenge his self-proclaimed alpha status, something Michael had no intention of doing. But the mere sight of the other boy's cocky smirk set Michael's teeth on edge. If Donnall was spoiling for a fight, Michael was in no mood to disappoint him. He'd be damned to the Shadowlands before he'd meekly roll over and play the omega.

"Seeing as how tomorrow's the big day, I just wanted to give you my condolences."

The three boys snickered and elbowed each other in the ribs.

"But then I thought about it," Donnall went on to the amusement of his followers. "And I figured it might be all to the good. While we're at it, we ought to burn the lot of you. Why waste time on another trial? If you ask me, the Singletons ought to be forbidden to breed altogether. Save us the bother of having to get rid of 'em later."

Michael's fist connected with Donnall's face before he had time to check the impulse.

"Nobody asked you," he snarled.

Blood spurted from a gash above Donnall's left eye, and he staggered back, then came up swinging. Michael ducked, catching the blow on his right shoulder. The fight ended with both boys bleeding and panting on the ground. Michael glanced up and saw Ivan James and the Medicus, *Simon Kendrick looming above them, looking less than conciliatory.*

Ivan grasped Michael's arm, and hauled him to his feet. Simon did the same to Donnall, then leaned down to examine the deep gash through the boy's left eyebrow. Ivan grabbed Michael by the shoulders, turned him around, and herded him toward the schoolhouse.

"What in the name of Corvus has the two of you at each other's throats again?" Ivan demanded, shoving Michael roughly through the narrow doorway. "Sit," he ordered, pointing one bony finger at the nearest bench.

Michael sat. A few moments later Donnall entered, followed by the Medicus, *who steered the other boy toward one of the benches on the opposite side of the room. Donnall held a thick square of cotton to the cut above his left eye. His right eye, shooting daggers at Michael, promised retaliation if it was the last thing he ever did.*

"This one'll have to be sewn up a bit," Simon announced. "But I reckon he'll live. What about you, Singleton? Looks like you gave worse than you got."

Michael's bruises had already begun to fade, and he felt the familiar tingle of cuts and scrapes knitting themselves back together. He shrugged, and tried to avoid the Medicus' *scrutiny by letting his long hair fall forward to cover his face.*

"What do you boys have to say for yourselves?" Ivan asked sharply, hands planted firmly on his narrow hips.

Michael kept silent. In part, because he had no good excuse for his behavior, but also because it was hard to tell which of Ivan's questions were rhetorical, and which were not. Donnall scowled his displeasure, but kept silent as well.

Ivan clapped his hands in dismissal. "All right then, boys. Have it your way. I don't have time for this now. We'll deal with it later. Simon, take Donnall home and stitch him up."

"I'll make sure Innes knows what happened," Simon assured the older priest. "That ought to take care of Donnall. Not really sure what's best to do with Michael, though. Seems to me, Branden's got enough to worry about, so as it is. Might want to wait until after..."

Simon let the sentence trail off, cleared his throat, and looked down at the floor. Ivan nodded grimly.

"Let's go, Maxwell."

Simon grabbed Donnall by the elbow and dragged him through the door. When they were gone, Ivan turned his attention to Michael. The hair on the back of Michael's neck prickled — a warning, perhaps, that Ivan was trying to probe his mind. Michael's response was automatic: he quickly erected a shield around himself, hoping the barrier was strong enough to keep a senior Guardian from sensing his thoughts.

A moment later, out of the corner of his eye, Michael noticed the deep frown etched into the old priest's forehead. He breathed a quiet sigh of relief, *and waited patiently for Ivan to pronounce his sentence.*

Dust motes danced in the light streaming through the small, square window. A woodpecker hammered, just outside the opened door, loud, staccato bursts; the dissonant beat of an unskilled drummer struggling to keep time to the melody of thrushes chirping in the boughs above. Voices faded into the forest, as the class headed home to prepare for the next day's celebration.

He was familiar with the anticipation everyone was undoubtedly feeling as they readied to celebrate the birthday of the god, Tempus. Gatherings were always a big deal, but this year, the mere thought of what was going to happen made his stomach clench in knots of dread and horror. While a part of Michael was glad to see Uncle Jared finally get what he deserved, another part couldn't help feeling as though the council was making a terrible mistake. He knew it was a sin to doubt, but he couldn't help it.

The priests said that cursed males were an abomination, that they offended Corvus, and should be banished to the Shadowlands. But what was being done to Jared just felt wrong, *despite all he'd been taught by the priests about Sacred Law.*

Then again... it might only be his own future he worried over. How many could boast that they knew exactly how—*if not, when—they were going to die? Though simply knowing a thing wasn't the same as watching it play out before your eyes. Would Uncle Jared scream? Michael figured he probably would. After all, how could he help it? The smell would be the worst of it, he thought. If he could stand that, he could probably stand the rest.*

Ivan James, hands clasped together in front of him, rocked steadily back and forth on his heels. If Michael didn't know better, he would have sworn the usually unflappable teacher was nervous about something. Maybe the pending execution weighed heavily on old priest's conscience. It must be no small thing to vote in favor of killing a man, no matter his crime.

Ivan cleared his throat, jarring Michael back to the present.

"Rest assured, your father will hear of this incident—and the others, as well. Our patience for childhood games is wearing thin, Michael. The Sacred Order will not continue to look the other way. You and Donnall are young men now, not children. It is time to start acting like it."

The warning in Ivan's voice was clear. Michael mumbled a hasty, "Yes, Honorable Guardian," then rushed out the door before Ivan could warm to the lecture.

Too late for fishing, he decided with a glance toward the sky. The sun was now hidden behind a patch of thick, gray clouds, and pleasure seemed to have inexplicably lost its allure. Michael ducked into the forest and took off running as far and as fast as his legs could carry him.

* ~ * ~ *

He would not *drink it. There was no way he was going to.*

Seamus used his right shoulder to pin Michael against the wall, and tried to force the wine past his lips. Even with his mobility hampered by heavy chains, Michael managed to knock the cup from Seamus's hand. With a dull crack, it landed on the hard stone floor.

Seamus swore vehemently. "Don't take it too much to heart that I said I admire yer spirit, Singleton," he muttered, getting up to retrieve what was left of the wine. "I ain't gonna put up with bullshit. Donnall says give you the drink, I do it. Up to you whether I do it the hard way or the easy way."

Panting heavily, Michael leaned his head against the moss-covered wall. He looked up at Seamus, his eyes pleading for mercy—for *reason*—from his childhood compatriot. Panic constricted his airway, making it more difficult than usual to force the words out.

"Listen, Seamus, you don't have to do this. Donnall's order didn't come from the Captain."

Painful coughing racked his body. Beads of sweat trickled into his eyes, and he thought his teeth might crack from the violent way his jaw was chattering.

Seamus shrugged, picked up the cask, and poured another dose into the crude, wooden goblet. "Makes no difference. Orders are orders."

Donnall's voice boomed through the mouth of the staircase. "You should have stayed in the land of the *advena*, Singleton. I always figured you for a freak of nature. Now everybody knows the truth."

He strode briskly to Seamus's side, glanced down at the cask and the still—full goblet. "Hurry up," he ordered. "The others are right behind me."

"He won't drink the wine," Seamus complained, with an irritated glance at Michael. "Spilled the first draught, so I had to pour another."

Donnall ground out a curse, grabbed the goblet from Seamus's hand, and stalked toward his captive. "Open up, Singleton, 'fore I have to knock them fucking misshaped teeth down your throat!"

"Illchangesmeinto," Michael whispered, voice harsh and raspy, sounding as loud as a scream to his ears. *" 'Every n—night and every m—morn... S—some to m—misery are born.' "*

He took a deep breath, cringing as his muscles swelled and contracted. *"S—sweet delight. Endless n—night..."*

But the chants weren't helping. He'd suppressed it too long. *Bestiae* was awake, and desperate to break free. His hands clenched into tight fists. A groan of helpless frustration was torn from his throat. His vision blurred, and he blinked rapidly in an effort to clear it. He felt his bones shift, and he cried out from the agony of it, desperately trying to control the responses of his traitorous body.

His nails sliced deep into the skin of his palms. His nostrils flared, scenting blood.

"Ill..."

Deep breath. His head lolled drunkenly from side to side.

"...changes..."

His tongue barely able to from the words, they sounded more like growls than human speech.

"...me..."

The pain was unbearable. He was going to die this time, he knew it. Though if — by some miracle of Fatum — he did not, his jailors would no doubt make him wish he had when they discovered the creature replacing the man they'd captured. His flesh burned from the inside out. Every nerve in his body screamed in protest.

"...into."

* ~ * ~ *

The drums began to beat at dawn's first light. Michael crept through the fog behind Mystery Hill, his heart pounding in time to the rhythm, his eyes burning from lack of sleep, his limbs sore from running all night through tangled vines and wild underbrush. He heard raised voices coming from inside the stone chamber beneath the altar, growls and snarls and curses, the sounds of a madman fighting the Inevitable.

The Inevitable would win, no doubt, but Michael figured Uncle Jared could not help but rebel against his fate. It was not in Jared's nature to accept what was being done to him. Perhaps it was not in anyone's nature to go calmly and willingly to a fiery death—no matter what the gods decreed.

Hidden from view by overgrown foliage, Michael peered through the leaves as the gathering commenced. His eyes watered as smoke tinged with the pungent scent of burning wolfsbane invaded his mouth and nose. In keeping with the Ritual of Execution detailed in Sacred Law, large bundles of the plant were being heaped onto the firepit. Michael wondered how the people so close to the bonfire were able to stomach it. The smell was nauseating, even from far away.

The sun had fully risen above the ring of mountains by the time the council—dragging a thrashing, growling, bound and helpless Jared Singleton—emerged from the Oracle Chamber. Uncle Jared's matted hair and unkempt beard, coupled with the torn and filthy state of his clothing, only aided in the perception that the Sacred Order had rightly judged their prisoner a madman, a danger to himself and others.

Michael's father, the Honorable Guardian Branden Singleton, led the procession up the rise of the hill, to the bonfire. The throng of people gathered round the firepit retreated. A hush fell over the crowd as Branden raised his arms in supplication, and began to recite the sacred prayers.

With every word that fell from his Guardian's lips, Jared's curses grew louder, and his struggles more frantic. He screamed as they dragged him closer to the fire, begged the council to have mercy on his soul, vowed to spend the remainder of his days chained up in the dungeon, if only they would spare him the horror of being burned alive.

The priests ignored his desperate pleas. They circled the prisoner, and began chanting softly in the tongue of the ancients. Their voices gradually grew louder, mixed with the steady beat of the drums, and seemed to vibrate along with the standing stones. Michael broke out in a cold sweat. His heart hammered against his ribs.

Corvus have mercy, they were actually going to do it! Somehow—he wasn't quite sure why—Michael had convinced himself that his father would save

Uncle Jared at the very last moment, that Branden would somehow be able to persuade the council to spare his brother's miserable life. But when Branden leaned down and slid his hands beneath the prisoner's armpits, it was obvious that he had no intention of doing any such thing. The Honorable Guardian of the Dead, Claudius Andrick stood opposite Branden. Michael watched, frozen, as Claudius bent down and took hold of the prisoner's feet.

Jared's ankles and wrists were shackled together by two short lengths of sturdy chain. His neck was collared in iron, the collar attached to a chain which had been wound around his upper torso and locked securely at his waist. They had not gagged the prisoner, though they probably should have. His howls were primal, viscerally shocking. Michael recognized the song. It was older than time, carved deeply upon his soul.

It was the song of the Beast that still lived within them all.

With an effort, Michael stifled the urge to howl along with his uncle, but others watching the spectacle had no such inhibitions. Some cried, some screamed, some pleaded for Corvus to spare them the horror. Men wept openly. Mothers covered their children's eyes. Babies wailed above the crackle and hiss of the colossal fire that reached thirty feet or more above the circular pit. And through it all, the tribe continued to chant the sacred verses to the rhythm of the drums.

The other priests assisted Branden and Claudius in lifting Jared, who appeared out of his mind with fear and rage. He thrashed and squirmed, snarled and screamed and sobbed, but the priests were not moved to so much as look at him. The seven robed figures stared straight ahead, lips moving as they chanted along with crowd.

Michael tried to look away, but was riveted by the scene unfolding before his eyes. Shadows crept around the edges of his vision. His mind went blank, and his body shut down, functioning just enough to keep air moving in and out of his lungs. He felt weightless, insubstantial, disconnected. Moments before, there had been solid earth beneath the soles of his scuffed, worn boots. Now it was quicksand sucking him deeper, deeper into the abyss.

He gripped the end of a sturdy branch to keep from falling over. The world swam in and out of focus. Everything moved in slow motion, like a dream. Sounds were muffled, distorted. The priests took a collective step forward, then heaved their burden into the roaring flames.

The screams were excruciating. But something was wrong. The cries for help were not, Michael realized with a sickening sensation of horror, the prisoner's alone. His keen hearing detected another voice entwined with Jared's in the Song of Death. Hungry flames rapidly devoured the unexpected feast, as the priests stumbled over each other in their haste to rescue one of their own. Michael couldn't tell which priest had accidentally fallen into the firepit, but it seemed unlikely he would be pulled out alive. No one could reach the man without risking being devoured by flames, himself.

Seconds passed. Then minutes.

Too long, too long, too late, Michael thought. He spotted Aunt Stella, running towards the firepit. She *was shouting something. Something that sounded like...*

No. Please. No.

Corvus have mercy, it can't be—

"BRANDEN!!!"

Hours later, Michael hadn't moved a hairsbreadth from his hiding spot. Strong winds blew over the standing stones, sweeping clouds of black smoke toward the distant mountains. Still, the stench of burnt flesh and wolfsbane lingered in the air, as did the melancholy echoes of death's song. The melody played over and over inside his head. Wouldn't stop. Wouldn't stop. It was going to drive him mad.

He watched as they pulled two charred bodies from the smoldering embers, listened as they theorized about what had gone wrong. After a heated debate by the remaining seven members of the Sacred Order, the final consensus was that Branden's robe had gotten caught in one of the chains, and the momentum had hurled him into the firepit along with Jared. Michael figured that was as close to the truth as they were likely to get. But what did it matter? His father remained dead, either way.

He wasn't quite sure why he didn't feel sad, didn't feel devastated, didn't feel... Anything. He had loved his father. And despite everything Jared had done, Michael had loved his uncle, as well.

Hadn't he?

"It is a tragedy beyond measure to send an honorable Guardian into the realm of Venefica," commented Ivan James from his perch atop a log, a few feet from the firepit. His lean, weathered face was

smudged with soot and ashes, and there were blackened smears on his long, brown robe.

"Brothers, I am begging you. Please reconsider opening the portal for one of our own. Branden died in service to his god, performing his sacred duty to Corvus. Surely, such a sacrifice should earn him the right to dwell in the glory of the Otherworld, not condemn him to everlasting torment in the Shadowlands."

"But once the door has been opened," argued a haggard, soot-covered Claudius Andrick, "I cannot control which soul passes through it. And I cannot, lest I forswear my sacred vows, risk allowing a cursed man's soul to pass into the Otherworld."

"What would Corvus consider the greater sin?" argued Corin Alexander.

"The cursed are an abomination," said Simon Kendrick. "An affront to Corvus. Sacred Law tells us they should, under no circumstances, be allowed to enter His kingdom. If we dare to disobey Sacred Law, we will surely feel the wrath of His vengeance."

The debate continued through the night, and into the early hours of the following morning. In the end, the council was unable to come to a consensus. The honorable Guardian of the Dead, Claudius Andrick, was the only priest with the power to open the door to the Otherworld. He was, therefore, given final authority.

The door remained closed, and the spirit of the Honorable Guardian, Branden Singleton was condemned to wander the Shadowlands for eternity.

Branden's only son, in turn, was condemned to a lifelong obsession with finding the door to the Otherworld, as well as the key that would open it.

Second only to a powerful aversion to fire, Michael's greatest fear became banishment to the realm of Venefica—the everlasting torment of the Shadowlands.

CHAPTER FIVE
Break On Through

Alena Andrick
Blackwater Hills

I huddled in the darkened corner, frantically trying to come up with a plan to get out of the basement before anyone saw me.

"Seems like a sacrilege to treat Branden's son this way," I heard Innes say.

"Well, that'll teach him a lesson 'bout messin' with the daughter of the Guardian of the Dead," Donnall replied angrily. *"Cessio, vappa ac nebulo.* Seamus, by the blood of Corvus, get a hold of him, man!"

I heard the scrape of iron across concrete, frantic shouting, growls and snarls—followed by an earsplitting howl, unmistakably animal in nature. The sound vibrated in my bones, like biting on metal. My teeth clenched involuntarily, and the hair on my scalp and forearms tingled. Heavy footsteps pounded down the staircase. Rusted hinges screamed, and my ears rang with the clang of iron on stone as the heavy cell door slammed against the wall.

"Donnall, watch out!"

"AHHHHhhhhhhhggghhh!!!"

Horrific screams mixed with menacing growls. I heard shouting, frantic footsteps, agonized cries. I raced through the archway, toward the door of the cell.

The sight that greeted me over the threshold froze my blood. I heard a roaring in my ears, like the swollen Blackwater River, and the metallic tang of fresh blood assaulted my senses. My knees buckled, and I leaned against the wall to keep from falling over.

The door to the staircase had been closed and bolted. About ten feet to my left, the iron door to the cell hung open. Just outside the cell, lay Innes Maxwell's motionless body. The floor beneath him was covered in a spreading pool of blood. Traces of it, like bright red paint, splattered the walls and bars of the cage.

A tight semicircle of guards partially blocked my view of an animal—what appeared to be a cross between a bear and a large, furry wolf. The creature was crouched in the corner of the cell, snarling ferociously.

I told myself it had to be shock distorting my vision, because there was no way I was actually seeing that huge black beast. No way. *No way.* It was simply not possible.

Gods of earth and sky.
Where is Michael?

Then the guards drew in closer, blocking the animal from my view. Every instinct I possessed screamed at me to run, and without another moment's hesitation, I obeyed. With a speed I wasn't aware I possessed, I darted past the cell, lifted the heavy iron bar, and flung open the door to the staircase. As my foot landed on the bottom step, the room behind me exploded into chaos.

I looked over my shoulder in time to see a blurry, black shape rushing toward me. With a startled exclamation, I flattened myself against the door. A fraction of an instant later, I felt silky fur brush against my legs as the animal raced through the open doorway to the top of the stairs.

Four guards charged up the stairs after the beast. I followed, stopping just beyond the landing to catch my breath. I caught a glimpse of the entry hall. The heavy, plank door stood open; one by one, the guards raced through it, and were halfway across the meadow by the time I got outside.

I spotted Malcolm Maxwell near the edge of the forest. He raised up a bow, and began firing off arrows, one after another. One of them hit its target, and the animal went down, close to the tree line. A few seconds later, it scrambled up on all four paws and darted into the shelter of the forest. The guards followed, disappearing through the wall of trees and tangled undergrowth.

Panting heavily, I sank to my knees. Wave after wave of dizziness washed over me. Nausea roiled in my gut, and I swallowed convulsively.

It seemed an eternity before I was able to stand, seemed to take a tremendous effort to get my legs to work properly. I walked slowly back toward the castle in a daze, and found Mother standing at the top of the basement staircase. I'd never seen her look so frightened before. Her attention seemed fixed on something on the floor below her.

Mother backed up a few steps, to let Sayla Kendrick came up the stairs. Sayla wrapped her slender arms around my mother's stooped shoulders.

"Is he dead?" Mother whispered, her voice filled with so much raw grief it was painful to hear.

"Sit you down, Cora," answered Sayla, gently. "Pray that Corvus guides his spirit to the glory of the Otherworld."

* ～ * ～ *

The Sacred Order, by a unanimous vote, elected Donnall Maxwell to serve in his deceased father's position as Captain of the Guard. My half-brother's first order of business was to command the guards to track down Michael, whom he referred to as, "That savage creature! A murderous abomination!"

His second, was a formal request to the Sacred Order to waive the Evaluation and impose the death sentence immediately, rather than the usual custom of waiting for the nearest sacred gathering day—the summer equinox, more than three months from now.

The Sacred Order remained characteristically taciturn on the subject of Michael's execution (and now pointless Evaluation), and had sequestered themselves upstairs in their private meeting chamber to debate the issue. The guards had spent the better part of the day and evening out combing the forest, but so far had found no trace of beast nor man.

I'd be lying if I said I wasn't glad Michael had escaped, but that didn't mean I was glad that my mother had lost her *lifemate.* Sayla Kendrick and I remained by Mother's side throughout the remainder of the afternoon and into the evening, but when Sayla said her good-byes and left us alone, I felt awkward and inadequate, unsure how to help—not even sure I *could* help.

My mother and I sat across from each other at the kitchen table. Mother's hands were rigidly clasped in her lap, her wide shoulders slumped, head bowed. I wondered if she was able to sense how guilty I felt. Though I knew it made no sense at all, I wondered if she thought I was partly to blame for what had happened to Innes.

"I think I'll make tea." I jumped up and headed toward the woodstove, anxious to have something to do with my hands. "Would you like some?"

"Gratiae, no," she replied in a careworn voice. "I should go back to my cabin and try to rest, like Sayla said."

"It's too far to walk, alone. And it will be full dark soon. Why don't you go upstairs to the guest room and lie down for a while?" I suggested.

She nodded, but made no move to get up. I busied myself making the tea, then carried the mugs to the table.

"Just try a little," I coaxed as I sat back down. "It's peppermint. Your favorite."

Her face took on a wistful expression that was quickly replaced by a bewildered sadness. She reached for the mug I'd placed in front of her. Awkward silence settled over the table, and I sipped my tea, wincing as the steaming liquid scalded the tip of my tongue.

"The castle feels different, somehow," she said, after a few moments. "Not really like home, anymore."

Home.

The word reverberated in my head, as I puzzled over what she'd meant. Mother and Innes had lived in a tidy cabin about an hour's walk from here. But the castle was her home, in the sense that it belonged to all the children of Corvus. It did feel as though the echoes of Innes's violent death lingered in the air. As though the castle had a memory, was affected by events as much as the people within it.

"Twenty-seven years, Alena. It isn't enough." She lifted her head, and her eyes blazed with the force of her emotions. "Still, I have one consolation: I know my son will avenge his father. Donnall will not rest until the abomination is destroyed, and the Balance is restored."

Tears burned my eyes, but I stubbornly refused to let them fall. Mother never welcomed much comfort from anyone, rarely asked anyone's assistance, was consistently levelheaded and wise, capable of finding the solution to any problem. At least, that's how I had always thought of her. She was the most selfless person I knew. It was rare to see Cora Maxwell without her mantle of serene optimism. Rarer still, that she opted for spite or revenge when the course of forgiveness was an option.

"But maybe it wasn't..." I blurted out without thinking. "I mean, you don't really think that Michael—"

"Members of the guard testified to being present when the change occurred. Donnall watched that vicious animal slaughter his father. And there's something else I've been meaning to ask you about. I didn't want to mention it with Sayla here. You know how she likes to carry tales. But earlier, I overheard Malcolm Maxwell swear that shortly after the attack, he saw you open the basement door and run up the stairs. I doubt he's suggesting that you intentionally let the beast escape, Alena." She fixed me with a look of gentle reproach. "But it did make me wonder what you were doing down there."

"I was...uh... Praying," I stammered, seizing upon the first excuse that popped into my head. "At the altar in the sanctuary. Father gave me permission to use it."

Mother sighed, apparently accepting the lie. Then her gaze turned inward. When she spoke again, she seemed to be talking more to herself, than to me.

"Your father and I debated this issue so many times. I thought the cursed ought to be given a chance to prove themselves. It seemed logical to believe that not all of them would die from the disease. Some of them, yes. The ones whose minds were infected were the most dangerous. But some of the cursed seemed to be able to control it, and did not appear to be mad at the time of their executions."

The image of the skull in my backpack flashed through my mind. Chasing its heels was the echo of Michael's deep, raspy voice: *I can control it, Alena. Don't be afraid.*

"Claudius always replied that the Evaluation set forth in Sacred Law was the only sure way to determine whether a male was deserving of execution. That the disease was fatal for all of them, it just progressed more slowly in some. Your father believes Sacred Law holds sway over the laws of man. He's a priest, and from the perspective of a priest, anything that is not his magic, sanctioned by his god, is evil or a sin. I would have expected no less.

"But the irony is, that although their family has produced more cursed males than any other family in the tribe, it was the Singletons who argued most vehemently in favor of execution. Their family motto, *Mutare Sperno,* speaks quite clearly their views on the subject. Now, in light of what's happened to Innes, it's beginning to make sense."

"What are you talking about?" I asked, hopelessly confused, for I knew too little of the family history of the Singletons.

Mother shook her head, as though shaking herself to awareness, then glanced over at me as though she had forgotten I was there. "A story better left untold," she replied sadly. She stood up and carried her mug to the sink. "It's getting late. We both should try and get some rest."

I stood up, hugged her goodnight as she passed by, then watched as she shuffled through the archway and disappeared from view. A few moments later, I took a deep breath and looked around to make sure I was alone.

I swung the long strap of my backpack off my shoulder, undid the buttons, and cradled the ancient skull in my hands. My fingers caressed the dry, yellowed surface as I wondered about the man whose mind had once lived inside. Had he been a Campbell, Andrick, MacDonald, Alexander, Kendrick, Singleton, James, or Maxwell? The man could have belonged to any of the eight families of the clan— including the Singletons, despite their current negative opinion on the subject of their ancestry.

Mutare Sperno.
We Scorn To Change.

CHAPTER SIX
Jonathan Speaks/A Treatise On Plausibility

J. Lance Sr.
Blackwater Hills

"*It's getting worse every day. I've tried everything I could think of to get it to stop, and nothing works. I don't know what else to do.*"

Jonathan stared intently at his nephew, alert for any signs of... Well, he wasn't sure what he was looking for, exactly. Whatever it was, he didn't find it. Michael looked the same as he always looked: like an impossibly handsome, exceptionally physically fit, twenty-one year old man. Except, perhaps, a bit more tired than usual.

Jonathan sighed, gathered up the pages he'd been working on, and set them aside. "A mantra might help," he suggested casually.

"*What's a mantra?" Michael asked. "And how do I get one?*"

"*It's a word or phrase that you chant during meditation. The objective is to clear your mind, open yourself to spiritual revelations and nonsense of that sort. As to how you'd get one, make one up. Who'll know the difference?*"

"*Have you ever tried it?*"

"*Good Lord, no. Thinking's difficult enough, without spiritual revelations getting in the way.*"

Michael took a deep breath. Held it. Exhaled slowly.

"Well then, perhaps there are some medicines that might help your..." Jonathan waved his hand in the air, as though by doing so he could somehow summon the correct terminology. "Condition. You can't go trying to treat your ailment without knowing precisely what it is. I mean, do you think a doctor could—"

"No. I don't. It would be way too risky." A tense silence invaded the room. Michael closed his eyes. His jaw clenched in agitation.

"It's just... I don't know, Jay. I was just thinking that there has to be a way I can open the door by myself. The cure is there, in the Otherworld. I know it," he insisted. "I have to go back to Blackwater Hills."

Jonathan dismissed Michael's threat to return to his birthplace. He'd been hearing versions of that threat since he'd married Michael's aunt. Truth be told, he was finding it—and the entire conversation, for that matter—a bit hard to take seriously. And who could blame him? Even for someone in Jonathan's profession, it was rare to hear a man confess to believing that he suffered from lycanthropy.

"What about an anagram, then?" he suggested.

Michael's eyes slid open. "What?"

"Take your name, for example, rearrange the letters to spell something else, and use that as your mantra. We used to do it to our teachers, in University. Mr. Harold Samuels, professor of history, became A Humorless Lad. It described him perfectly. My personal favorite was Mrs. Theodora Bold, who taught English. Her name spelled Hot Old Broad. Couldn't call her that to her face, of course."

Jonathan opened the top drawer of the desk, took out a pen and a crisp sheet of paper, lowered his head, and began to write.

A few minutes later, he lifted his head and smiled. "A Lion Neglects Him. Change Time, Ill Son." The smile grew wider. "Oh, this is a good one: Till Change Is On Me."

Michael looked skeptical. "You got all that out of the letters in my name?"

"You've got a good name for this sort of thing. There are a lot of vowels to work with." The pen scratched against the paper, then Jonathan held it aloft in triumph. "I got it!" He exclaimed. "Ill Changes Me Into."

"Oh yeah, that's perfect," Michael muttered, looking disappointed. "Is that the best you can do, Jay? I don't think it's going to work."

Jonathan nibbled on the end of the pen. "It's quite remarkable, actually. The fact that those words are even in there, I mean. Think about it: Ill—or, sickness—Changes Me Into. The tribe claims it's a disease of some sort, don't they? And change could mean any number of things. Changes in personality. Changes in behavior. And, of course, the more obvious change: man into—"

"What time is it?" Michael interrupted, hastily.

Jonathan glanced at his watch. "Eight-thirty. When do you have to be to work?"

"The usual. Five a.m.. Not that it matters how early it is, cause I can't sleep anyway."

"Drink hot chocolate. It works wonders, believe me."

Michael nodded, absently.

Jonathan toyed with the pen, sliding it back and forth between his thumb and index finger. "You know, it isn't necessary for you to work, Michael. My last two novels sold very well, and I could hire you on as my assistant, or something."

"I don't mind. It helps me focus."

"Another key to unlock the imaginary door?"

"I don't know," Michael mumbled. "Maybe."

"In that case, you could take care of the gardens and general repairs. There's plenty of manual labor to be done around here. The lumberyard is no place for a man like you.

"Just think about it," he added, when Michael didn't reply. "As for this door business... Do you know where the tribe originated?"

"Germany, Scotland, different parts of Europe, and North America. What does that have to do with anything?"

Jonathan shrugged. "I don't know. Have you ever thought that there might be another cause for this disease, some other explanation for why it happens? I mean, it's not unheard of for people to carry genes specific to their race. And because the tribe has kept themselves isolated for so long, they don't have access to modern medical care."

Jonathan tapped the pen on the desk, and rubbed his chin with his other hand. "You're looking for some kind of spiritual door, because you think the answer—the way for you to control this disease—is behind it. In other words, you're suggesting that the Spiritual controls the Physical. Do you really believe that's possible, Michael?"

"I would like to believe," Michael answered, "that anything is possible."

Jonathan sighed. "I'd like to believe that, too. I don't know why I can't."

$$* \sim * \sim *$$

Despite his choice of profession, Jonathan Lance was not a superstitious man. A self-described atheist, he had never given credence to things otherworldly—least of all, werewolves. He had never considered the possibility that they might exist outside the confines of myth and pulp fiction. Until, that is, the moment he saw Innes Maxwell's ravaged body laid out on a pallet in the Great Hall of the castle.

Outside the drafty castle windows, dusk descended into night. Inside, Jonathan tiptoed around Innes's lifeless body as though his every step might trigger a land mine. Like a movie that's so bad you can't stop watching it, his mind replayed the nightmare of the past few days. His hands began to tremble. He curled them into tight fists and shoved them deep into the pockets of his overcoat. Part of him stubbornly clung to the hope that there was a sane, rational explanation for what had happened to Innes Maxwell. An explanation that had nothing do with the fact that Michael was a werewolf—because *that*, logic insisted, was impossible. There was such a thing as mass hysteria and, he reasoned, that was undoubtedly what was going on here.

But then, he was forced to ask himself, what manner of creature tore this man's flesh to ribbons and chewed a ragged, bloody hole in his throat? Where was Michael? Why were his clothes found shredded on the dungeon floor, and how had he managed to free himself from iron shackles without breaking the locks?

Huh, Mr. Logic? Can you answer that?

Like an incessant reminder of the horror, the sour, metallic smell of blood lingered in the air. Jonathan could almost feel it, like a heavy burden weighing on his shoulders. And once the image of Innes's torn, bloody flesh had burned itself indelibly into his brain, Jonathan knew he would never again doubt what his nephew was capable of.

His stomach churned. Bile stung the back of his throat. Gagging, he whirled away from the body. He stumbled to one of the long, wooden benches lining the walls, and fell onto it before his legs gave out entirely. He cradled his aching head in his hands, as he chanted under his breath,

"This is not happening. This is not happening. This is not happening.

"This is not happening.

"This

"Is

"Not

"Happening."

Jonathan lifted his head and stared blankly at the shadows that draped the wide, arched doorway like a velvet curtain. He nearly jumped out of his skin as the girl materialized slowly through them. The waning fire in the hearth lit her mane of reddish-gold hair, while light from the wall torches flickered in her dark brown eyes. Jonathan recognized her immediately: Alena Andrick, the girl Michael had run off with the night of the celebration.

According to Jackson Singleton, Alena was Innes Maxwell's nineteen year-old stepdaughter. She was the product of an adulterous affair between Innes's wife, Cora, and Claudius Andrick—a priest with the dubious title of Guardian of the Dead. Like the parents of a teenage girl out too late on a date, Jonathan and Jackson had sat up all night worrying and waiting for Michael to return. Jonathan had been forced to listen to Jackson drone on and on about who was related to whom (as in, Anna Andrick begot Allistair, who begot Claudius, who begot Alena). But he'd never gotten the chance to ask Michael what had really happened, for Michael had been captured and arrested on his way back to Jackson's cabin.

"Oh," said Alena, looking startled when she noticed him there. "It's you. The *advena.*"

Outsider.

Definitely.

"Call me Jonathan," he said, trying to appear as though he wasn't about to have a nervous breakdown any second. Noting the weak, thready sound of his own voice, Jonathan cleared his throat and tried again.

"I just came to see... That is, I thought they might have... found him."

"Not yet." Even, white teeth flashed as she nibbled on her full lower lip.

Jonathan wasn't sure whether he was relieved or disappointed with her answer, but a streak of panic went through him nonetheless. What the hell was he supposed to do now? Even if he could somehow find his way out of Blackwater Hills, he couldn't leave Michael to the mercy of these barbarians and their primitive Sacred Law.

"Jonathan, are you all right?"

Alena's pleasant, lilting accent jerked him back to the present. He nodded curtly, and stood up.

"Fine," he muttered, as he headed for the door. "I'll go now. Sorry to have bothered you."

"Wait," she said. "Can I talk to you for a moment?"

Curious, he turned around. An elastic silence crept through the Great Hall, pulling and stretching his mind in all directions. Jonathan became mesmerized by the shadows writhing and twisting on the young girl's porcelain skin. As he stared, she shifted her weight from one small, booted foot to the other.

"Are you going to look for him?" She blurted out, finally.

He heard a note of anguished desperation in her voice, and wondered again what had transpired between Michael and Alena. Michael had obviously not hurt the girl. Not in any way that was evident physically, at least.

Had the two slipped into the woods for a romantic interlude? Did Alena Andrick have feelings for Michael? Assuming they managed to find Michael before the guards did, would Alena be willing to help get his nephew safely out of Blackwater Hills?

Hope flared briefly before Jonathan reminded himself who she was. Alena Andrick was the daughter of one of the most powerful priests in the Sacred Order—and the stepdaughter of the man Michael was accused of murdering. It might be a mistake to trust her.

He gave a short bark of anxious laughter. "The thought crossed my mind, but I don't have a clue where to begin looking. I'm not from around here, as you may have noticed."

She shifted her gaze around the room, then leaned in and whispered, "I think I know where he might be hiding. If you promise to get him safely back to the land of the *advena,* I'll take you there."

"You traitorous bitch!"

The accusation thundered in Jonathan's ears. His heart lurched into his throat as Donnall Maxwell stormed into the Great Hall. The newly-elected Captain's face burned with bright red blotches—signs of passion or anger, Jonathan guessed. It was either that, or the man's head was about to explode.

To Jonathan, it seemed as though Donnall was always shouting—even when he was silent. When Donnall Maxwell was near, it was difficult to focus on anything else. Everything about the man demanded attention. An air of restless anger banished calm the moment the Captain stepped into a room.

Alena looked startled, but seemed to recover more quickly. "I wasn't asking your permission," she retorted with a defiant lift of her pointed chin. "I don't *need* your permission."

"In the name of Corvus, do not interfere with this Evaluation, or I swear, I'll—"

"Drunk with power already?" She practically spit in his face. "You can't stop me."

"As Captain of the Guard, I have the ear of the council," he shouted back. "And Malcolm saw you open that door. It's because of you, that the creature escaped. I'm sure, diligent student of Sacred Law that you are, you understand what that means."

"You're lying," she said.

Donnall looked smug. "He's already said he will testify."

Alena arched delicate eyebrows mockingly. "You'll have a hard time convincing the Guardian of the Dead to side with you against his own flesh and blood."

Donnall swore under his breath. "I'm warning you, Alena, if you try to protect Michael Singleton, you will tangle yourself in vines even your father cannot extract you from. Those vines have thorns. Don't play games with me."

Even at the worst of times, Jonathan was a writer, and was unexpectedly impressed with Donnall's metaphor; it was a trifle clumsy, but it made its point. Alena responded by making a face at the Captain—a gesture that reminded Jonathan how young she really was. From what he could glean from the motley collection of barbarians he'd met thus far, Alena seemed to be the only one who did not believe Michael deserved to be executed. Even Jackson Singleton did not seem willing to offer help—choosing instead to remain in the shadows, taking it all in but never voicing an opinion. The rest of the tribe were out for Michael's blood. It seemed to Jonathan, he had no choice but to bet on the supposition that Michael and Alena had formed some sort of bond, however tentative.

He didn't want to think about the consequences of betting on the losing side, but thought Alena's reaction to Donnall's opposition looked promising. The young woman's air of fragility owed more to her outward appearance than to her personality, he discovered as he watched her argue with her half—brother. Auburn hair and the face of a mischievous angel hid the soul of a warrior, for what other kind would have the courage to stand up to the explosion-waiting-to-happen that was Donnall Maxwell?

Did she do it for Michael? Or were there currents beneath the surface that Jonathan could not even begin to fathom? Donnall and Alena certainly appeared to strongly dislike each other. There was a story here, but most of the pages were missing. Jonathan wondered if any of the missing pages contained vital information, something that might affect the outcome of Michael's story—and his own.

He didn't want to dwell on that, either. He was an outsider. An *advena.* He wanted to fade into the background, didn't want to attract the wrong kind of attention. After seeing what they had tried to do to Michael, one of their own, Jonathan realized it would be a very bad idea to rub these people the wrong way. He was afraid, however, that by conspiring with Alena Andrick, he may have already done so. Donnall did not appeared pleased, in any case.

The Captain stalked menacingly toward him. Jonathan fought an embarrassing urge to duck behind the table. Then, the most surreal moment he ever experienced, happened: Donnall Maxwell loomed over him—long brown hair flying out in all directions, green eyes glinting with hundreds of tiny sparks like fluid circles, breaking apart and swirling back together...

It's only a reflection of the torch light, Jonathan told himself frantically. *Only actors in bad horror movies have eyes like that.*

Despite this universal truth, Jonathan felt himself tumbling headfirst into the void of the Captain's swirling, sparkling gaze. He collapsed upon the bench, as though shoved backwards by a strong but invisible hand. Chest heaving, he struggled to breathe. Alena's innocent, heart-shaped face peered around the Captain's shoulder.

She rolled her eyes. "I could do better than that against a human," she sneered. "Give it up, Donnall. I doubt he's impressed by the pathetic display of your limited abil—"

The Captain backhanded her across the mouth, sending her flying halfway across the room. She crashed in a heap upon the stone floor, her face hidden in a mass of reddish-gold waves.

"Learn to control that mouth of yours, sister," he snarled, whirling around.

Alena scrambled up an instant later, and leapt onto the Captain's back, clawing at his face and tearing at his hair. With a muffled curse, the Captain reached around, grabbed a handful of her baggy flannel shirt, and flung her off. She landed only inches from the mauled body of her stepfather. Donnall towered over her, his powerful chest rising and falling rapidly, his classically handsome features twisted in a mask of fury.

"You know where he is, don't you?" The Captain's deep voice was pitched deceptively low. His only obvious flaw, the scar bisecting his left eyebrow, stood out in sharp relief against his flushed skin. "If you don't tell me right now, I'll have you arrested."

Alena dismissed the warning with a scowl, at first. A fraction of a second later, it seemed to dawn on her that it was no idle threat. Her face paled. She climbed awkwardly to her feet, as Donnall moved toward her. He backed her up against the wall, then his right hand shot out and closed around her throat.

"Tell me where he is," he demanded. "Or by the gods, I'll make you regret the day you were born."

"Rot in the Shadowlands, *vappa ac nebulo,"* she choked. He clipped her on the cheek with his other hand. Her head smacked against the wall. He let go her throat, grabbed her left arm, and twisted it up behind her back.

"Tell me where he is!"

Alena cried out in pain, and struggled against his punishing hold. She kicked his legs and clawed at his arms, but her efforts were ineffectual against his greater strength. This was no fair fight; Donnall was a full foot taller than his sister, and outweighed her by eighty pounds, at least. Broad-shouldered, and lean with muscle, he had no trouble subduing his obviously weaker, female adversary.

Though desperate to go to her aid, Jonathan's mind swam in a fog of dull lethargy. His limbs felt numb and heavy, and he found that he was unable to move no matter how intently his brain willed his body to obey the directive. Panic surged through him. He tried frantically to come up with a plausible explanation for what was happening. Tried without success to convince himself that it was only fear holding him captive, not Donnall Maxwell.

Because *that,* Logic insisted, was impossible.

No other interpretation withstood careful examination of the facts, however, so Jonathan was forced to concede that Donnall might have used some sort of mind-control trick on him. How the Captain had done such a thing, Jonathan hadn't a clue— though it could be some kind of hypnosis, he reasoned. All Jonathan knew of hypnosis, was that it was a useful and convenient plot device when one had carelessly written oneself into a corner. He'd never actually experienced non-fictional hypnosis.

So there
It is.
A logical
Explanation.

"What in the name of Corvus is going on in here? Donnall, let go of your sister this instant!"

Cora Maxwell bustled into the room, and headed straight for her grappling, snarling offspring. She placed one hand upon Donnall's chest, and shoved. Donnall released his grip on Alena, who dropped to the floor holding her throat. Narrow shoulders rose and fell, as she tried to catch her breath. Donnall backed up, alternately glaring at his mother and sister.

He thrust a finger accusingly in Alena's direction. "She knows where he is! She's hiding the abomination!"

"I'm *not!*" Alena tossed the hair from her face, dabbing gingerly at the bleeding cut on her mouth. "Mother, he tried to *kill* me!"

Cora planted both hands firmly on her ample hips, and fixed them both with an impatient scowl. "Won't you two ever grow up?" She demanded. "You ought to be ashamed of yourselves, carrying on like this, after everything that's happened. Alena, let me see how badly you're hurt. Do you need the *Medicus?*"

Alena shook her head no. Cora held out a hand to help her daughter to her feet, then took a step back to survey the damage. Alena's right eye was swollen and just beginning to turn purple. Her lip was cut, her pointed chin streaked with blood. She winced as she rubbed her abused wrist, which had already begun to swell.

"Don't worry about me," she answered hoarsely. "See to the *advena*. Donnall has put him under *captare.*"

Cora shuffled over to the bench, and appraised Jonathan critically. "Donnall," she commanded, an edge in her voice that promised to entertain no argument. "Release him at once."

Donnall muttered something unintelligible under his breath, then turned around.

"Stay out of this, Alena," he growled, before disappearing around the corner. "Consider that your first—and only—warning."

Alena crossed the room to stand beside her mother. "Are you all right, Jonathan?" she asked.

The genuine concern in her eyes surprised him. He nodded as he pushed up from the bench, relieved to once again have control of his own body. His legs shook so badly, he was afraid his knees would buckle and send him crashing to the floor. Cora held out a hand to steady him, but he waved it away.

"I'm fine," he mumbled. "Sorry to have bothered you. I—I should go..."

Neither woman made a move to stop him as he stumbled toward the front door. Once outside, he leaned against the outer stone wall of the castle, and inhaled deep lungfulls of the cool night air. He gazed across the meadow to the dark wall of trees. Stars winked above the circle of snowcapped mountains in the distance, while locusts and cicadas assaulted the night with discordant harmonies. Michael was out there somewhere, he realized, wounded and alone, being hunted like a rabid dog, or an aggressive mountain lion.

Or like the animal he really is: the creature who killed Innes Maxwell.

Jonathan's throat constricted, and his heart pounded an unnatural beat upon his ribcage.

Get it together, Normal Man, his mind insisted. *Figure a way out of this.*

"Oh, fuck," he sobbed, dropping his head in his trembling hands. There was no way out of this. None that he could see, at any rate. His only option was to make his way through the pitch black forest to Jackson's cabin, then sit there and wait until Michael either came back on his own—which was highly unlikely—or was captured and brought back in shackles and chains.

Assuming, of course, that they brought him back alive, for Jonathan knew it was more likely they'd kill him as soon as he was found. Alena Andrick had offered Jonathan his only hope of finding Michael before Donnall's guards did. Jonathan needed her help. Without it, he was left to venture into the forest alone to find Michael. Or, failing that, try to find his way back to the car he'd left parked miles away on the dirt road at the edge of the forest.

But, according to Michael, Jonathan would not be able to get through the Great Shield on his own, and would need someone with the blood of Corvus running through their veins to lead him through. Jonathan recalled how he had scoffed at the idea of an invisible shield protecting Blackwater Hills from outsiders. He had teased Michael mercilessly about it the entire journey from Ashland. But now... What did it matter now? Bruised and battered, her brother's warning ringing in her ears, Alena was probably having second thoughts about helping the *advena.*

On shaking legs, he stood up and stumbled awkwardly down the winding stone path. He crossed the wide, moonlit meadow, and headed blindly into impenetrable darkness.

* ~ * ~ *

Jonathan spent a good hour or more wandering lost in the forest, before Alena Andrick stepped through a wall of trees and tangled undergrowth, like a specter rising from the misty gloom.

After the beating Donnall had given her, Jonathan had assumed she had changed her mind about helping him. But the warrior's soul he'd had a glimpse of earlier in the evening was out in full force, primed for battle. To thwart her half—brother, it seemed Alena was determined to rescue Michael before the guards found him. Jonathan was still a bit leery of putting his and Michael's lives in the hands of a mere slip of a girl he barely knew. But when it came right down to it, what choice did he have?

They trudged for miles through the overgrown wilderness before coming upon a tiny cabin that Alena said Michael had built himself. Familiar with Michael's skill with a hammer and nails, Jonathan found it hard to believe his nephew was the author of such a crude, dilapidated structure, until Alena explained that Michael had been twelve years old at the time. After a thorough search of the cabin and surrounding grounds found the place deserted, they went inside to rest and plan their next move.

Alena wanted to wait for Michael to return to the cabin, but Jonathan was desperate to get out of Blackwater Hills, and safely back home to Ashland. As was his habit since losing his wife, Stella, less than a year ago, Jonathan searched his pockets for a joint and a book of matches. The weed did not completely relax his addled nerves, but it did manage to subdue the anxiety swarming in his gut like a pack of angry bees. After taking a few hits from the joint, he offered it to Alena. She stared at it as though it were a snake about to strike, then declined the offer with a shake of her head.

"What is it?" she asked.

"Marijuana. Have you ever tried it?" Jonathan extinguished the glowing ember, and dropped the roach inside his coat pocket.

She shook her head. "What does it do?"

"Takes the edge off. You know, like a pint of beer or a shot of whiskey."

She nodded understanding. "Like ceremonial wine."

"Something like that," he said with a dry bark of laughter. "But I never could abide wolfsbane, myself. Talk about side effects."

An awkward silence descended. They had opted to light the only candle, even though Alena was afraid that even such meager light flickering through the grimy windows might betray their location. Jonathan studied Alena through the gloomy shadows, wondering how she was faring after the beating she had taken at the hands of her half—brother earlier in the evening. She hadn't once complained of her injuries, which puzzled him. It was as though she was neither surprised nor particularly offended by the violent way she'd been treated. As though she believed Donnall had every right to threaten and beat the shit out of her.

Though, for all Jonathan knew of this backwards society, Donnall did have that right. Not wanting to remind her that he was little more than an ignorant *advena,* Jonathan nonetheless needed to make sure she was not hurt. He asked, and she hesitated before admitting that her wrist still ached and her blackened eye was becoming painful.

He stood up, walked over, and knelt by her side. "Let me take a look."

Gently, he peeled back the sleeve of her flannel shirt. She tensed, but didn't pull away. More by touch than sight, Jonathan determined that her wrist and right eye had swollen to nearly double their size. The cut on her lip had scabbed over, but looked as though it could have used a couple of stitches to keep it from breaking open again. Considering the size of her brother and her brother's temper, the damage could have been worse. It was the swelling that worried him.

"Is there cold, running water nearby?" he asked.

"I've got a waterskin in my backpack, if you're thirsty." She answered.

He shook his head. "Not for me, for your wrist. To get the swelling down."

She did pull away, then. "It's okay," she bit out, jerking the sleeve down to cover her hand. "I've had worse."

He was startled. "From Donnall?"

She shrugged.

"Alena," he prodded, "has he done this before? Why doesn't anyone stand up to him, stop him from abusing you? He doesn't have the right to hurt you, you know. Doesn't your father—"

"It's okay," she interrupted, an edge in her voice. "Father says Donnall and I bring out the worst in each other, and he's right. But Donnall hardy ever hits me anymore. Only when I provoke him, which is why Mother's always telling me to control my mouth. I can't help it sometimes, though. Just being around him makes my skin crawl."

"Well, no wonder!" Jonathan exclaimed, unable to mask his outrage. "They've allowed him to abuse you, and have somehow convinced you that you deserve it for provoking him. You poor girl."

Alena clearly did not want his sympathy. Her lips tightened, and her pointed chin jutted at a stubborn angle.

"Sorry," he muttered. "It's none of my business."

"Parvi refert," she said, after a few tense moments. "And just so you know, I've read a lot of books. I know things are different in the land of the *advena.* But here..." She shrugged again. "We live by the laws of Corvus."

"There's such a thing as moral law," Jonathan countered. "Don't your people have a sense of right and wrong?"

"A different one than your people have. That doesn't automatically make ours inferior."

"I never said it did."

"But it's what you were thinking."

Jonathan was disconcerted and a bit embarrassed by how easily Alena Andrick had managed to read him. Then again, he'd often been told he possessed an expressive countenance—and she did have the advantage of not being stoned.

"Can you read minds, then?" he asked, an edge in his voice.

"A little bit," she answered. "Sometimes."

He raised an eyebrow, unable to mask his skepticism. "Oh, really?"

"Yes, *really.* What's so odd about that?"

When he did not immediately reply, it seemed to occur to her that reading minds might not be as common in the land of the *advena* as it was in Blackwater Hills. One brown eye—the one that wasn't swollen shut—widened.

"Can't you?"

Jonathan cleared his throat, and searched her face. She looked sincere, but deep down, he sincerely wished she had only been amusing herself at his expense.

"Can all descendants of Corvus read minds?" He asked, avoiding the obvious question and its myriad implications.

"Some are better at it than others. Stronger, I mean. Males who are cursed are said to have the greatest powers — even more than a Guardian. But most of them are unable to find the Balance, and never learn to properly control it. It drives them mad, and they become violent, dangerous."

"Find the Balance? Michael says that all the time. What does it mean, exactly?"

She gazed at him with an eye that evinced a rare spark of intelligence, was suddenly too bright, too perceptive. The floorboards groaned in protest as he shifted uncomfortably under the scrutiny.

"Have you ever seen Michael when he...?" she faltered, unable to come up with a suitable word to describe Michael during one of his episodes.

"It's the madness," she resumed, a few moments later. "Little by little, it eats away at their minds. The beast gradually consumes the man, until all that's left is an animal trapped in human form. Their bodies are *immutabilis*—incapable of the transformation from man to beast and back again. It makes them wild and vicious, like rabid animals. The perversion of His power greatly offends Corvus. He considers it an abomination, and it is by His decree that cursed males are put to death."

Unable to come up with a suitable reply, Jonathan digested her words with the acid of mounting anxiety.

"That's why they're after Michael, in case you were wondering."

He heard a note of resignation in her gentle, lilting voice. Her shoulders slumped as she burrowed deeper into a pile of blankets and pillows.

"So," he asked, a bit unsteadily, "do you agree with the Sacred Order? Do you think Michael deserves to be executed?"

"I don't know what to think. The priests tell us it's a sin to question Sacred Law, but I can't help wondering if they only say that because..."

"What?" he prompted, when the silence seemed to go on too long.

She shook her head. "Nothing. It doesn't matter. No one listens to me, anyway."

"I'll listen," offered Jonathan, settling into his own nest of blankets and pillows. After all, it wasn't as though he had anything else to do, and listening to

Alena's problems might help take his mind off his own. But instead of elaborating, she changed the subject.

"Are you and Michael very close?"

"I thought so." If there was any bitterness in his tone, it came from the realization that the man Jonathan thought he knew might not be the man his nephew really was. "Before we came here. Now... I'm not so sure."

"Because you think he killed Innes," she said, and he winced.

"That's part of it," he admitted.

"Do you believe he can transform?"

There was a note of curious excitement in her voice—not the fear and revulsion Jonathan expected to hear. Not the horror and disgust that he, himself, felt whenever he recalled the ravaged state of Innes Maxwell's body.

"Do *you* believe it?" He countered.

"There's no other way to explain the deformity."

The faintest of chills ran down Jonathan's spine. "What deformity?"

"You've never seen it?" There was a clear note of surprise in her voice.

"Never seen what?"

"His teeth," she explained. "You can't tell unless he smiles a certain way, and I'm sure he's mastered the art of shielding them by now. They're kind of like a wolf's teeth. Or a bear's. Hold on, I'll show you."

Alena reached for her backpack. She pulled out something round and solid—looking, and held it out to him. Jonathan's hands itched to reach out and grab it, but he curled them into tight fists instead. When she realized he wasn't going to take it, she lowered the object to her lap, and stared down at it thoughtfully.

"At first, I thought he was showing his teeth deliberately. To scare me. But then I realized he was trying to tell me something. When I found the other skulls in the tomb, I figured out what it was."

Jonathan knew what she was going to say next, knew he didn't want to hear it, because hearing it spoken in Alena's gentle, lilting accent might make him start actually believing it, and that would mean he had completely lost touch with reality.

"I realized that the shape of his teeth proved that he was able to make the transformation," she finished matter-of-factly.

"How'd you figure that?" He demanded, a little more harshly than he meant to.

"Four hundred years ago, the tribe began to breed with the children of Tempus. In as little as three generations, human blood weakened the blood of Corvus, and males began to lose the power to change their shape."

"What does any of that have to do with Michael's teeth?" Jonathan interrupted. The lesson in Tribe History was interesting enough, but he was anxious for her to get to the point. His nephew's life—and perhaps, his own—was at stake.

"Those who could change were not always reviled, you know. In the days before the Sacred Order, they were considered the true sons of Corvus, gods come to earth. After I saw Michael's teeth, I got to wondering. Maybe when a male changes his form, his teeth are the only part of him that doesn't fully recover. According to Sacred Law, any such abnormality of the teeth is considered grounds for execution, for it proves beyond a doubt that the male is cursed."

"So, other men of the tribe have had this... this deformity?"

"Not like Michael does. I've heard of some that have had a few extra molars, or sharper than normal canines, but Michael has a full set of everything, exactly like the skulls in the tomb."

"And you think that proves he can change into a wolf?" Jonathan asked, feeling sweat break out beneath his armpits, despite the chill that permeated the cabin.

"Bestiae," she corrected. "A *beast,* not a wolf. But... yeah."

Jonathan's mind reeled drunkenly. His heart missed a beat, then took up a disconnected rhythm. From the corner of his eye, he was vaguely aware of Alena peering at him curiously.

"Jonathan? Are you all right?"

"Fine," he muttered, feeling sick to his stomach. His hands shook, as he groped for the roach in his pocket and lit it hurriedly. He exhaled a cloud of pungent, silvery smoke, and watched it swirl lazily around his head.

"Are you hungry?" she asked. "I brought along some food."

When Jonathan left Jackson's cabin to look for Michael, food had actually been the last thing on his mind. But at the mention of it, his stomach began to rumble impatiently. He nodded, and she began to rummage through her backpack. A few minutes later, she produced two loaves of bread, a large jar of sweetened apple-butter, a giant hunk of yellow cheese wrapped in green cloth, some dried meat, and a canteen of spring water.

After they ate, Alena packed the leftovers away and they settled into a companionable silence. Images of Michael flashed through Jonathan's mind. He pictured Michael wounded and possibly dying, alone in the forest, crying out for help. He was anxious to find him, but feared that finding Michael might be the easy part.

How does one go about rescuing a werewolf?

Jonathan thought that he really should have seen it coming because, after all, this was a standard, bottom-of-the-barrel horror plot. He cursed himself for a blind, stupid, disbelieving fool.

And you call yourself a Genre Novelist. Ha! What an Oxymoron.

Eventually, the candle melted into a puddle of wax atop the overturned crate, and worry and exhaustion claimed their due. Jonathan settled into his mound of pillows and musty wool blankets, and drifted into a fitful sleep.

CHAPTER SEVEN
To the Other Side

Michael Singleton
Blackwater Hills

Michael opened his eyes, then winced as the bright rays of sunlight slashed through gaps in the budding branches overhead—seemingly with the intent of boring holes through his eyeballs. He closed his lids, but the light continued to assault him. It burned through his right thigh, just below his hip. Pain flared through every cell in his body—thousands of tiny spasms, dancing tongues of fire that felt as though they were trying to torment him to death.

Or maybe I'm already dead, and death hurts like a son of a bitch.

He laid on the muddy ground and tried not to move. It was quite some time before he discovered that the sun was not the cause of his excruciating pain. The culprit was an arrow—poisoned, no doubt—protruding from a good sized hole in his flesh. The shaft had broken off about a foot from the wound, and was stained and crusted with dried blood.

He rolled over, and tried to push himself up. Panting from the exertion, he shook his head like a wet dog, then collapsed against the nearest tree. His fingers lightly probed the wound in his thigh. The arrow needed to come out, but right now it was acting to staunch the flow of blood. He had nothing to use in its place, for his clothes had been left in the cell with his man-form. He had regained the latter without much difficulty, but knew the former would be somewhat harder to obtain.

"Shit," he muttered.

His skin was covered in deep scratches and dark, ugly bruises—the majority on his hands and forearms—causing him to wonder what the hell he had been doing. Though he suspected the effort would be futile, he searched his memory, attempted to piece together what had happened after the change. Someone had obviously intended to either slow him down or kill him. But who? *Why?* And how had Michael managed to escape?

Not Michael, he reminded himself. *Bestiae.*

And he won't tell you what happened. He never does.

Michael wasn't sure when he began thinking of the creature as a separate entity—could not recall the moment they had come to a tentative agreement to share one body. Not that Michael really believed he had much choice in the matter; *Bestiae* would take what he wanted in the end, anyway. But the compromise had made things a whole lot easier, allowing him to hold onto his man-form for longer periods, and making the inevitable transition much less painful.

But now, as always, it drove him near-crazy to think about the specifics of the transformation. Logic demanded that the act itself ought to be impossible. For despite growing up with the legends and traditions of the tribe, Michael had embraced the science and ideas of the humans he'd lived with the past ten years. He'd been enamored of the idea that magic was a myth, enchanted by the notion that even gods were forced to submit to the laws of physics.

Corvus, apparently, was the exception that proved the rule. The Beast god had found a way to defy the laws, and had passed the secret on to his children. But the true son of Corvus was not the man, and for Michael, that realization had been the most devastating of all. Yielding control of his body and mind to *Bestiae* was never easy, but it was better than the alternative: *Blood madness,* a lethal infection.

Michael had long suspected that the disease was caused primarily by an inability to ascend to the Balance, and was not—as the Sacred Order preached—necessarily a result of the children of Corvus breeding with the children of Tempus. The priests who served the Sacred Order were partly to blame, as they had strayed too far from their original purpose—to protect the men who had inherited the power of the Beast god. As a result, without a Guardian to assist him during and after the transition, a gifted male was indeed dangerous—even deadly. It was because of this, that the laws of execution were necessary for the clan's survival.

Of course, understanding that did not make it any easier to accept. Especially because *Bestiae* would not let Michael surrender without a fight. And if the dried blood beneath his fingernails was any indication, Michael suspected that there had been a fight of some sort. In a contest between Beast and man, Michael was willing to bet *Bestiae* would emerge the victor.

Maybe now he could add murder to his list of transgressions.

He certainly did not intend to stick around and find out for sure—even if it meant walking on the injured leg. Pain could be tolerated. Imprisonment and execution could not. Standing proved more difficult than he'd anticipated, though he managed it after several, teeth-grinding attempts. For what felt like an eternity, all he could do was cling to the rough bark of the tree, and try to catch his breath.

The forest blurred disconcertingly. Michael began chanting, softly. The familiar ritual brought forth some small bit of strength when he feared he had used his full reserve, kept him from succumbing to the darkness seeping round the edges of his vision.

As his tongue tripped clumsily over the words, he was aware of the thick, jagged quality of his voice—something that seemed to worsen with every change. The pressure of a headache throbbed against his temples.

" 'Every night and every morn
Some to misery are born
Every morn and every night
Some are born to sweet delight
Some are born to sweet delight
Some are born to endless night. '"

As the final verses rasped from his throat, renewed energy surged through his mind and limbs. Relieved that his body once again belonged to him, Michael rested his forehead against the rough tree bark, and tried to figure out what to do next. Returning to Jackson's cabin was not an option Michael wanted to consider, but he was naked and wounded in the middle of unfamiliar forest; it was unlikely he'd make it to the nearest town in his condition.

And there was Jonathan Lance to consider, as well. Michael couldn't abandon Aunt Stella's *lifemate* to the fickle hospitality of Blackwater Hills. Not simply because Jonathan was human, more because of his connection to Michael. There was a very real possibility that the tribe would turn on him.

Michael lifted his head and scanned his surroundings. Trees. More trees. And more, after that. He had no clue which direction to take. Panic rippled through him. As he wrestled it down, a raven alighted on one of the branches just above his head. The faint rustling of leaves seemed to echo in the stillness of the forest. Then the bird tilted its head to one side, opened its sharp beak, and began squawking loud enough to wake the dead. Michael winced as the discordant notes sliced through his skull. A moment later, came another large bird, then another, then one more.

Four beady pairs of eyes examined him critically. Then all four birds began chattering at once, as though involved in a heated debate. The noise gradually increased in volume. A wave of dizziness washed over Michael. Splinters dug beneath his fingernails as he tightened his grip on the tree, desperate to keep hold of the only solid object left in the world.

The ground roiled and twisted like the deck of a ship. He felt the scrape of rough bark on the palms of his hands, felt his body slowly sliding downward.

"Cessio, Prince. Do not fight us."

Surrender.

Michael thought for sure he was losing his grip on reality, for it seemed as though the words had come from the beaks of the chattering birds. They flew from their perches and fluttered around his head, landed on his shoulders and squawked in his ears.

"Cessio, Prince. We have come to help you."

Michael groaned, as his head hit the ground.

Rescued by blackbirds? Fever, he thought. *I must be delirious.*

* ~ * ~ *

"You shouldn't have brung him through the door. It's against the Law."

The voice was loud, reminiscent of tires crunching over gravel. Michael's first impulse was to cover his ears, but he couldn't make his hands obey the weak directive. His mind felt numb and hazy, like the aftereffects of ingesting too much ceremonial wine. He felt as though he had been buried neck deep in wet sand. Moving—even the slightest bit—was impossible.

"Well, I wasn't about to leave him there so those crazy priests could kill him. You think Raven would rather we'd done that?"

"No good going off and deciding on yer own, is all I'm saying."

"We were on a scouting mission. You know how those things are, Mack. About as exciting as watching flies fuck. Which, by the way, is all there is to do, cause don't nothin' ever happen. I figured we could bring him through while he was out of it, patch him up real quick, and then send him back. No harm done, and I can't see as how Raven can object to that."

"I'm sure He'll think of a reason," grumbled Gravel-Voice.

"Well let's hurry up then, before He finds out."

"What are you, Justin? An idiot? Ye can't keep nothin' from Raven. He's *all knowing-all seeing,* remember? Best stick to that story about wantin' to save this puppy's miserable life, and hope he goes easy on ya. But make sure to leave out the part about the flies. Wouldn't want the Captain to think you're a slacker."

"I don't care what Captain Arren thinks. He's had it out for me ever since I joined the patrol. That last incident wasn't my fault, and he knew it, but he holed me up in the brig anyway—for fifty years! You know what somethin' like that does to a person? Do you have any idea the shit that goes on in there?"

There was a long silence. Michael felt rough hands touching his body.

"Captain Arren claimed he did it for my own good, to 'build my character.' Bullshit, I say. He just plain don't like me, and that's a fact."

"Then what'd you go and do somethin' so stupid for, if you know the Captain has it out for ya? Come on, help me get him up on the table."

"I was just perched up there in that tree, watching him, and something came over me. I can't really explain it, but all of a sudden it hit me how fucked up it is for the Princes nowadays. That Sacred Order crap changed everything. Things sure ain't like how they was when we were alive, Mack. I'm just glad I died before all that shit started. Imagine having to deal with *Bestiae,* and all them crazy priests wanting you dead at the same time—knowing there's no way you can win against either one. I felt sorry for the kid, Mack. Shit, don't you?"

"A little," Gravel-Voice—aka Mack—conceded. "But if Raven doesn't share your sympathy, you might find yourself back in the brig quicker'n you can blink."

Justin grunted in reply. "Move your arm over this way. Fuck, he's heavy."

Michael felt himself being lifted, carried, and then deposited like a load of timber upon a rough, hard surface. *Wood*, he deduced, by the splinters digging into his bare back. The hands took hold of his arms and legs, shifting his body's awkward position. He would have cried out had he been able, for with every movement, white-hot shards of pain blazed through his right side.

"The wound ain't so bad," Justin observed, dispassionately. "A clear shot to the muscle, but it looks infected. Poisoned, probably."

"What are you, a *Medicus,* too?" Snorted Mack good-naturedly. "Just pull out the shaft, and stitch him up. Even if it is poison, we don't got any salve to treat it."

"Camus had to report in, but he said he's gonna bring some back with him."

"You told Camus!" Mack's shout was like a well-aimed rock, straight at Michael's forehead. "Who else knows, Justin?"

"Camus helped me bring him through the portal. So did Nicholas. And Sage. You didn't think I was able to do it on my own, did you?"

"*By the blood of Corvus,"* Mack grumbled. "Are you trying to get us all thrown in the brig with ya?"

"Relax, Mack. They can't lock us all up. They need all the scouts they can get right now."

"Yeah, I guess you're right." Mack sighed. His fingers probing in the wound sent tongues of fire roaming through Michael's thigh. "Which is a good enough reason for keeping this pup alive."

Michael heard the faint creak of rusted hinges. The fingers kneading his flesh abruptly stilled. Silence reigned for a few torturous moments. Michael held his breath as the pain subsided, and then made another failed attempt to move of his own volition.

"What's going on in here, Justin? Why wasn't this reported? Raven demands that you surrender the prisoner at once."

"He ain't a prisoner," Justin hurried to explain. "He's a *Merula,* Captain, and he's wounded. See? Damn crazy priests were trying to kill him, so we brought him through the door."

"On whose authority?" Demanded the captain. "Scouts can't transport without permission. You are there simply to observe and report your findings, under strict orders not to interfere in the lives of mortals."

"I—I know that," Justin stammered. "But he was hurt, and I figured Raven would want us to keep him alive, so I—"

"Took it upon yourself to break order," interrupted the Captain. "Justin the Hero, is it?"

"No, Captain. I only thought—"

"That was your first mistake. Don't think next time. Raven wants to see you in his chamber. *Immediately.*"

"But what about him?" Justin asked.

"Heroism *and* loyalty? You're doomed, Justin." The captain heaved a heavy sigh. "I'll be in charge of the prisoner from now on."

"I told you, Captain, he ain't a prisoner, he's a *Merula.* Make sure you get a *Medicus* to treat his wound. It's infected with poison."

"We'll take good care of your pet," the Captain assured him. "Keep Raven waiting any longer, and he'll be the least of your worries."

* ~ * ~ *

Michael was more or less certain he was not dead.

He drifted in and out of consciousness. The pain in his leg had subsided, but it was taking a tremendous effort to keep his eyes open for any length of time. He began taking stock of his faculties. His heart beat, steadily. His lungs expanded and deflated with each in and ex-halation. His empty belly growled with hunger, and his throat felt parched from lack of water. The air felt neither hot nor cold, and he smelled nothing but the musk of his own sweat. Furthermore, the spacious, utilitarian chamber and the roughneck men who occupied it, did not bear the least resemblance to Michael's concept of the afterlife.

Michael watched through half-closed eyelids as the two men stalked round each other like tigers in a cage. The room was empty of man-made objects— except for the cot on which he lay, and the coarse, wool blanket covering the lower portion of his body. The walls, floor, and ceiling were made of a dark gray material that looked like concrete; they appeared smooth and solid, and were devoid of any doors or windows. Neither man possessed candle or lantern, and Michael could see no electrical devices or outlets. Nonetheless, the room was infused with a soft, white glow.

"You *had* to go and piss Him off, didn't you?" Mack—the larger of the two men—grumbled through his matted beard. "You couldn't keep your mouth shut, just this once."

Justin—tall and lean, with disheveled brown hair and a tangible aura of restlessness about him—glared at his companion, somehow managing to look angry, wounded, and betrayed all at once.

"I expected to hear that from Captain Arren and the rest of those bootlickers, but I thought I'd at least have you on my side."

Mack breathed a heavy, put-upon sigh. "He's Raven. You know, Lord and Master of the Otherworld and King of the Merula. I *have* to take His side, you clot-head, and so do you. Just admit you did the wrong thing when you brought this puppy through the portal, quit your whining, and take your punishment like a man. If you want the truth, I think you got off easy. You're lucky He didn't throw your ass back in the brig."

Justin scowled. "I wish He would have locked me up. Leastways, I'd be sure to come back. There ain't no way I can do this, Mack. It's exile to the Shadowlands, plain and simple. You know it. I know it. And Raven knows it, too."

Mack muttered a curse, and looked down at his fingernails. He examined them in silence, then lifted his head and gestured with his chin. "He's awake."

Justin nodded. "I know."

"Well, ain't you gonna tell him?"

"No." Justin slid his hands inside his trouser pockets, and began to prowl from one empty corner of the room to the other. "I figure, the less he knows, the better off he'll be."

"You can't plan somethin' like this, Justin. You just gotta go for it. Don't think about it too much, or you'll screw it up."

"It took four of us to bring him through the first time," Justin protested. "Even if I was able to do it by myself, it could be months before the portal opens again. Maybe even years! I can't keep him under *captare* that long."

Mack gazed thoughtfully at Michael's motionless body. "Well it won't be easy, that's for sure. Too bad there's no way to get them to open it sooner."

"Get who to open it? Raven is the only one knows how, and He already said He won't. He said He wants to teach me a lesson, so I think twice before I do something this stupid again."

Justin stopped pacing, and scowled at the wall. *"Teach me a lesson,* my ass. I know what He's trying to do. He's trying to get rid of me. He doesn't have the guts to send me to the Shadowlands Himself, so He's figured out a way to make it look like an accident."

"Calm down, will ya? I'm not talking about Raven. Get that crazy priest to do it. The Guardian of the Dead, I mean."

"How am I supposed to do that?" Justin scoffed. "The only time he opens the portal, is when one of 'em dies."

Mack slanted Justin a sly look out of the corner of his eye. Justin paled.

"Unh-uh." He shook his head vehemently. "No way. I ain't doin' that."

"Why not?" Mack argued. "It ain't against orders. I'd offer to do it for ya, but Raven said no one's supposed to interfere with your punishment."

"It's too risky, for one thing."

"Nah, not really. It's easier than you think. You don't even have to physically go there yourself. All's you have to do is spiritually possess one of 'em, and... Well, you know."

Justin's eyebrows shot straight to his hairline. Mack shrugged, crossed his thickly-muscled arms over his barrel-like chest, and leaned his back against the wall. Justin stared at Mack in incredulous silence for a long moment, then whirled around and began pacing again.

Though their voices had managed to penetrate the fog in his head, Michael was having a hard time following the conversation. *I'm dreaming,* he thought. *I am* not *dead.*

But what if he really *was* dead? What if his vision of the afterlife was totally off base, and this was what he had risked everything to find?

The Otherworld, Michael had always imagined, was an ethereal paradise in perfect Balance, where ultimate spiritual enlightenment was achieved simply by virtue of being there.

Obsessed with finding the door to the Otherworld since the moment he'd learned that the Guardian of the Dead did not open the portal for males who were cursed, Michael's greatest fear was that his soul would be left to wander in the torment of the Shadowlands for eternity.

Michael believed that he was powerful enough to open the portal, himself. All he had to do, he thought, was discover the secret incantation only the Guardian of the Dead was privy to. Nothing matter more to Michael than finding the door. It was the reason he had made the decision to return to Blackwater Hills and risk execution.

He couldn't believe his luck when he'd stumbled upon the key in the form of Alena Andrick. The fey little beauty had offered Michael the thing he most desired when she'd acted on her impulse to shield him during the feast. Though Alena's lesser power had not been enough to accomplish the task alone, by taking Michael under her protection, she had—albeit unwittingly—allowed him free access to her knowledge and memories.

Alena was not a Guardian yet, but the day would soon come when she would don her robes and pledge her life to serve the Sacred Order. Following tradition, the position of Guardian of the Dead was inherited, and the Andricks had held the title for five generations. Alena was Claudius's only child. Michael had been quick to recognize the possibility that Claudius Andrick had already passed the secret of opening the portal on to his daughter.

So on the night of the gathering, he had gradually allowed Alena's weaker shield to fade, then replaced it with one of his own making. Unbeknownst to Alena however, Michael had kept a firm hold on the psychic thread that linked her mind with his. As she slept, he'd stayed awake and searched her mind for the information he so desperately needed, and had been *so close* to uncovering the answer.

But probing another's mind was a delicate skill— one he'd rarely had an opportunity to practice, in the land of the *advena.* He should have listened when Alena had begged him not to return to Jackson's cabin, should have stayed with her in the forest until he'd uncovered the secret, but he'd thought he had plenty of time. He hadn't expected the Guard to arrest him so soon. After all, he had spent years learning to ascend to the Balance and ward off the blood madness, had been so confident in his ability to shield the deformity caused by his illness.

Idiot, he admonished himself. *Alena was right. Pride* does *goeth before a fall.*

He couldn't actually remember the fall itself, but suspected it had been a bad one. Now he was here—wherever here was—helpless and unable to move or communicate. The spell that linked his mind with Alena's had broken during the transformation, leaving him feeling hollow and alone in a way he had never felt before. His mind stubbornly insisted that the blackbirds who had "rescued" him had been nothing more than fever-induced figments of his imagination. Even though, despite the fact that Michael could not pick up a scent from either man, Mack and Justin appeared real enough. The motley pair could either be his saviors or his captors.

Michael had not yet decided which possibility was more likely.

The two men began walking slowly towards him. As they drew closer, a chill swept through Michael's immobile body, and his stomach knotted in apprehension. He was aware of their bodies looming over him, but still could not detect their scents—something that only served to feed his growing sense of unease.

No fear, he told himself. *I am* not *dead.*

"The *captare* comes and goes. Like, if I just concentrate on that, I can keep him under. But soon as

I pay attention to something else, he starts to slide out of it. I'm not strong enough, Mack. I ain't gonna be able to keep this poor pup alive until the portal opens again. What the fuck am I going to do?"

"Raven wouldn't have given the order if He didn't think you could do it, Justin."

"Raven must be trying to get rid of Michael, too," Justin retorted bitterly.

"He ain't trying to off you, man. Quit being paranoid."

"You're not helping, you know."

"I tried to help," Mack reminded his companion. "Ain't my fault you didn't like my suggestion."

"It ain't a matter of not liking it, Mack. I just don't want to kill anyone, that's all."

"Well, being alive ain't all it's built up to be. I don't remember my life being nothing to write home about, and from all the bitching and moaning I've heard you do, yours wasn't neither. Just pick some poor Captain who's getting ready to pass through the portal anyway. Like that cranky old priest, Ivan Something-or-other."

"It ain't for me to decide who lives or dies. What if I do it, and it upsets the Balance? Raven ain't going to take too kindly to that. I don't want to make things worse. I'm on shaky ground so as it is. I just want to get all this shit over with, and go back to the way things were before."

"Well according to you, it can't get no worse. You might as well use the only solution you got."

"I need to think about it some more," Justin answered. "Shut up, so I can figure out what to do."

Their deep, rough voices swirled through the fog in Michael's head like little white shadows—breaking up, then leisurely drifting back together. One word stood out above the rest, reverberating through his consciousness:

Captare.

The weapon of a Guardian.

So, that's what they had done to him. *Are they Guardians,* Michael wondered? *Priests of the Sacred Order?* Michael began to wonder if maybe he had dreamed the transformation. Or maybe the guards had found him while he'd lain unconscious in the forest. Had he been taken to the castle for the Evaluation? But if that were the case, why had they left him unchained? Upon his arrival in Blackwater Hills, Michael had made it a point to learn the names of every priest who served the Sacred Order. The names *Mack* and *Justin* had not been among them.

Michael struggled to rise above the spell he was under, tried to regain control of his body, but it was no use. The magic was too strong. Panic stirred inside him, and he ruthlessly tried to wrestle it down. Then, without warning, the fog curled back like a giant wave and crashed upon the shore of his mind, obliterating awareness and sending him spiraling helplessly through the ether.

No fear, his mind insisted. *I am* not *dead.*

CHAPTER EIGHT
Those Who Race Toward Death

Alena Andrick
Blackwater Hills

I sat up, brushed the knotted mass of hair from my eyes, and squinted through the grainy, pre-dawn light. Jonathan Lance was asleep beside the ruined fireplace, his body tangled in a pile of blankets, snoring loud enough to be heard in the land of the *advena.*

I wanted to believe it was only a matter of time before Michael showed up, but days had passed, and there was still no sign of him. I had been so certain we would find him hiding in his cabin, I hadn't planned on what to do if he wasn't here. Waiting seemed to be our only option, for I knew Donnall and the other guards were out combing the forest. The last thing I wanted to do was run into my brother—or one of his trained wolves.

I was beginning to think that Michael may have already passed through the Shield, and was on his way back to the land of the *advena.* Jonathan swore that Michael would never willingly leave him behind, but what if he had? Perhaps Michael had realized that his only hope of survival depended on getting out of Blackwater Hills immediately. He may have assumed that either myself, or Jackson Singleton, would help Jonathan escape.

That scenario sounded plausible enough, but I couldn't erase the memory of the poisoned-tipped arrow piercing the beast's hind leg as it raced across the meadow. How much damage had the arrow done? Maybe Jonathan *was* right. Maybe Michael was wounded, unable to travel, and we ought to go out and search for him. But if the search turned up a beast, not a man...

What would we do then?

I hadn't asked the question aloud, and neither had Jonathan. But it was what both of us were thinking. It was the reason we chose inactivity over action, when it was not in either of our natures to do so. The tedium of waiting, with nothing to do but worry and imagine the worst, had us both on edge.

I looked down, noticed that the swelling in my wrist had lessened, and I was able to blink my right eye with only minor discomfort. The damage to my pride, however, might take a bit longer to heal.

My stomach rumbled, and I reached for my backpack. As I rummaged through the pack, I dislodged the skull. The smooth, dry feel of it sent a chill through my body as it brushed against the back of my hand. Shoving the skull to the bottom of the pack, I grabbed the pouch of food, broke off a stick of dried meat and a small square of cheese, and then carefully replaced what remained of our dwindling food supply.

As I climbed to my feet, I swayed slightly, as though sleep had robbed me of energy rather than gifted me with it. A quick search of the room found the waterskin beneath a pile of discarded pillows, but only a few drops of precious liquid remained. I popped the last bite of cheese into my mouth, and decided a short walk to the river to refill the waterskin would ease some of the tension knotting my sedentary muscles.

Outside the cabin, the sun was just beginning to peek above the ring of mountains. The air tasted of crisp leaves, dry earth, and newly-hatched plants, was warm and clear, without the slightest hint of humidity.

On the way to the river, I thought about how good it would feel to bathe in the fresh, cool water. My skin tingled in anticipation, and I quickened my pace, pausing at the water's edge only long enough to remove my clothing. Stepping carefully over rocks and slippery moss, I held my breath, then plunged, headfirst into the icy water.

I came up, gasping for air, flinging my mass of sopping wet hair over my shoulders. For the first time in days, I felt refreshed and alive. Bright rays of sunlight warmed the top of my head. Trees crowded along the banks like an angry mob, their gnarled roots pushing and shoving to get closer to the water.

When my teeth began to chatter, I climbed out of the water, and tiptoed barefoot over the rocks to retrieve my clothing. I got dressed, refilled the waterskin, and then sat down to rest upon a smooth, flat rock.

The discordant music of the forest—the sigh of wind through the leaves, the chatter of birds, water trickling lazily around rocks and fallen tree limbs—helped ease the tension in my neck and shoulders. I rested my head on my drawn-up knees, and closed my eyes.

"Where is he?" A deep voice rasped against my ear.

I felt the tip of a knife against my throat, and fought the urge to start thrashing wildly. My limbs began to tremble uncontrollably.

"Careful, Alena," he warned. "I don't want to hurt you. But I will, if I have to."

Gagging on the odor of sour breath mixed with unwashed male, I slowly opened my eyes and caught a glimpse of shaggy brown hair and a face mostly hidden by an unkempt beard. It was Ian MacDonald, a member of the Guard, and the least abrasive member of the MacDonald clan. Though, that was really like saying a snowstorm was less intense than a blizzard.

I'd never had anyone hold a knife to my throat before, and the experience was more than a little frightening. I took in a deep, shuddering breath, and whispered, "I don't have a weapon, Ian. Put the knife away, and let's talk about this."

He frowned while seeming to consider the offer. As I waited for his decision, I had the oddest sensation. My body felt as though it was trying to grow larger, as though the vessel housing my soul had inexplicably become too small. It might have been fear that caused my vision to blur, as I watched Ian nod and straighten up slowly, knife held out in front of him.

I tried to raise my head from my knees, but it wobbled on my neck, too heavy to lift. Through the ever-darkening haze, I watched Ian lean forward again, felt his hand grip my upper arm.

"Get up," he ordered, but the words sounded thick and distorted. "And no funny business."

What happened next was nothing more than a blur of movement, obscured by the reddish haze of terror and a rush of adrenaline. I don't remember how I ended up on my back, clutching a bloody dagger in my hands.

Staring blankly up at the sky, I tried to breathe, tried to calm the nausea churning in my gut. Gradually, my surroundings came back into focus.

Too bright. Too *sharp.*

I closed my eyes. For what seemed an impossibly long time, I simply laid there and refused to open them. I resisted the temptation to look over at the body. If I didn't look, it wouldn't be real. The sticky warmth of his blood would not be drying on my hands. That sickening rasping, gurgling sound would not be the noise of a dying man struggling to breathe through a gash in his windpipe.

I sent out a silent, desperate plea to the gods, begging them to turn back time. Endless moments passed. The gods declined to answer.

The chattering of birds in the trees overhead gradually grew louder, drowning out the nauseating sound of the guard's labored breathing. I opened my eyes again. Tentatively balancing my weight on wobbly legs, I walked over and examined my vanquished attacker.

Don't be dead. Don't be dead. Don't be dead.

He wasn't.

But he will be soon, a panic-stricken voice whispered in my mind. *Get away from here, quick, before someone comes looking for him.*

I dropped the bloody dagger on the ground next to the body, stumbled away, and took off running back the way I had come. Halfway between the creek and Michael's cabin, I remembered the waterskin. I had left it on the rocks near the bank of the river, but it was too late now to go back and retrieve it.

I wondered if Ian MacDonald was cursing my name with his dying breath. If, in his final moments, my image was the one foremost in his mind. Then I deliberately thrust such thoughts away, buried them deep, and tried to forget the incident ever happened.

Think about it later. After the shock wears off. You're in no condition to deal with it now.

A short while later, the door to Michael's cabin came into view. The forest had tried its best to swallow the hideout, but parts of the dilapidated structure were still visible from a distance. Which meant that the guards were bound to find it, sooner or later. We needed another place to hide.

Sticky with the remnants of Ian's blood, my shaking hands were barely able to lift the door latch. Inside the cabin, dust motes danced on strips of hazy sunlight. It was a moment or two before they cleared enough to reveal Jonathan Lance sitting up in the corner. Bushy eyebrows raised as he looked me over. I saw his lips move, but couldn't hear the words through the sudden, loud buzzing in my ears.

He kicked aside the blankets, and climbed to his feet. Bold, masculine features morphed into an exaggerated expression of concern. His bright blue eyes seemed to grow larger and larger as he moved toward me. I'd never seen eyes that color before—the deep azure of the sky on a perfect summer day. He mouthed my name, held out his hand.

The world tilted. I felt myself sliding toward the edge, toward an abyss of nothingness. My last coherent thought was a prayer of thanks to the gods for having granted me a mercy I didn't deserve.

Then the darkness engulfed me.
Blessed ignorance.
Blissful escape.

* ~ * ~ *

Michael Singleton
Blackwater Hills

"You did it, Justin! They've opened the portal. Are you ready to go?"

"I ain't never gonna be ready, but I've got no choice. Might as well get it over with."

"Take your time, Justin. Trust your instincts. You can do this."

"Wish me luck. I'm gonna need it. Especially when the vacca ac nebulo makes his way through the portal and figures out what happened. You think he'll hold it against me, Mack? I swear I tried to make it look like an accident."

"Don't worry about it, man. My lips are sealed. Besides, he ain't a Merula, so there won't be any repercussions. Raven never did like Ian MacDonald much anyway."

In this space, time had no meaning. *Minutes? Hours? Days?* They were merely words, and Michael could not remember existing anywhere but in this hazy, shadowy netherworld of ghostly, disembodied voices.

Strong hands gripped Michael's shoulders, lifted him up, and gently guided him through the ether. His body felt weightless, less substantial than a cloud.

Justin's voice echoed inside his head: *"Steady, man. Don't screw this up, for once in your life. Do something fucking right, for a change."*

Then the pain began.

The change commenced without its usual warning signs, giving Michael no time to prepare for the agony of muscle, bone and sinew pulsing, twisting, and rearranging the body of a man into the form of a beast. Then back again, into man—form, but the transformation was happening too fast.

He was *falling,*
    falling,
        falling through a hole in the fabric of time and space, through the door connecting one world to another.

All that existed was pain and fear and Justin's unwavering presence beside him, guiding him through chaos. Though he feared that this was death—forever falling through the abyss, never landing—it was over long before Michael was aware that he was back on solid ground again, able to see, hear, think, breathe.

Every nerve in his pain-ravaged body screamed in protest. Ever so slowly, he lifted his head and looked around. Blood pounded in his temples, blurring his vision. Squinting against the glaring rays of the sun, he breathed in the comforting scents of living plants and clean, dry earth.

Michael's head dropped forward. He closed his eyes. Strength returned gradually, but it was a long time before he could sit, then stand, with only minor discomfort. He examined his naked body critically, and was shocked to discover that the wound in his thigh had healed cleanly, leaving no trace of a scar.

The surrounding forest was unfamiliar, but he sensed that he was once again within the Great Shield, in Blackwater Hills. He scanned the sky to pinpoint the direction of the sun: mid-afternoon, and the forest was bursting with life. A rabbit scurried through the underbrush, a few feet away. Michael dove after it, caught the squirming body in both hands, and snapped the animal's neck with one quick, practiced motion.

He used his sharp canines to tear the rabbit's soft fur away from its still warm body. When not a scrap of meat remained, Michael dug a shallow hole, and buried the bones and fur beneath a thorn bush. Licking the blood from his fingers, he stood up and went in search of water.

More than an hour later, he reached the banks of the Blackwater River. Sunlight sparkled and danced upon the surface of the water, making it seem somehow alive and magical. Michael immersed himself in the cold, rushing water, wishing it had the power to cleanse his soul as well. Aftereffects of the *captare* still clouded his thoughts, making them sluggish and difficult to process. A short while later, he climbed out of the river and continued walking.

He felt as though an invisible barrier, like a thick glass wall, had enveloped his mortal body. Sounds and sensations were muffled, distorted. He felt disconnected from the physical world, as though a part of his soul had been devoured by the ether, and was lost forever.

Maybe that was the price a mortal had to pay for passing, unharmed, through the door to the Otherworld. For, though the memory was rapidly fading, Michael was convinced that he had, indeed, traveled through the portal that connected the Physical world to the Spiritual.

If he could only remember how he'd done it.

He quickened his pace and broke into a run, crashing through the forest like a frightened deer sensing a hunter on his trail. Primitive, animal instinct took over. It rendered him oblivious to the thorns and branches scraping his skin, and silenced the voices inside his head—a feat even the *captare* had been unable to accomplish. Instinct obliterated the need for understanding. Awareness of self fell behind like a discarded mantle.

Michael Singleton did not exist.

Nothing existed but forest, trees, sky, and the rocky ground beneath his pounding footsteps.

CHAPTER NINE
The Law of the Forest

Alena Andrick
Blackwater Hills

A waning moon outlined the leaves and branches with shimmery, silvery light. Shadows crept like mist through the trees. Jonathan stopped a few feet ahead of me, his pace hindered by the thick undergrowth. Caught in a snare of prickly vines, he swore loudly and vehemently. He managed to extricate himself quickly enough, but not before sharp thorns claimed payment in flesh from his face and forearms.

The forest was impenetrable in spots, and fraught with hidden dangers. We'd spent all day fighting our way through it, stopping only once to rest and eat. When Jonathan remarked on our dwindling food supply, I couldn't bring myself to share his concern. I was an experienced hunter, I assured him. We wouldn't starve. Jonathan looked doubtful, but said nothing more on the subject.

Foremost in both our minds was finding Michael, but the search was akin to trying to locate the proverbial needle in a haystack. Compounding the difficulty, was the fear that we might run smack into one of the guards, or even Donnall, himself.

I wondered if I'd be arrested for the murder of Ian MacDonald. If I was found guilty of the sin of *homicidium*—killing without just cause—what would my punishment be? Murder was rare within the tribe, and each case was decided on its own merits. Although I couldn't remember what had happened, I believed I had acted in self-defense.

The question was, would the Sacred Order believe it?

I had known Ian my entire life. We were related, in a sense, for he was the older brother of Donnall's *lifemate,* Shaina. Ian had been somewhat less abrasive than his brother, Seamus. He had chosen a *lifemate* this past winter, and they were eagerly awaiting the birth of their first child—a fact that only served to intensify my guilt.

Wallowing in the mire of my troubled thoughts, I didn't even notice the ruckus, at first. Jonathan's shocked exclamation and hasty retreat alerted me to the presence of an intruder—by the sound of it, a large anima—crashing through the underbrush a few yards ahead of us. Motioning for me to be silent, Jonathan grabbed my arm, and guided me behind his back. With my sight partially obscured by his head and shoulders, I tried to peer around him to see what was going on. I got a glimpse of black hair, followed by a flash of tanned skin, before being shoved backwards. I tripped on an exposed root, lost my footing, and landed on my backside in a tangle of underbrush.

Jonathan fell on top of me. I heard growls and snarls and grunts of pain, was pummeled and kicked by flailing elbows and thrashing feet. Then the weight was lifted as though by magic. As my lungs heaved with the effort to suck back in all the air that had been denied them the last several moments, a familiar, rough voice cried out,

"Jay! What the hell are you doing here?"

"Looking for you!" Came Jonathan's startled reply.

I squinted though the deepening shadows. Michael crouched next to Jonathan, who lay sprawled on a bed of fallen needles at the foot of a thick pine tree. Jonathan sat up slowly, brushing leaves and debris from his hair. I followed his wide-eyed gaze as it swept over his nephew.

Michael was completely naked, tanned skin covered with cuts and abrasions, shoulder-length black hair a riot of tangled waves framing several days' growth of beard. His eyes appeared so dark, the pupils were indistinguishable. He looked feral and dangerous, and not unlike the large animal I had earlier mistaken him for.

I made a move to get up, and he turned his head, freezing my limbs with his gaze. My heart pounded an uneven beat upon my chest, and my palms began to sweat despite the cool air.

"Alena."

My name spoken in his husky, broken voice sent wave after wave of chills through my body. Fear rendered me immobile as he stalked toward me like a dark jungle cat advancing on his prey.

He reached for me. I scrambled deeper into the underbrush. He leaned down, grabbed my shoulders, pulled me up, and set me on my feet. His touch nearly made me jump out of my skin. Strong fingers slid down my arms and encircled my wrists. He took a step back and looked me over. His gaze halted on my face. He examined my bruised and swollen right eye, the cut on my lip that was not quite healed. Something in his expression made my insides quiver. Every nerve in my body hummed in awareness.

"Who did this to you?" He ground out, low and menacing.

He inhaled deeply, as though struggling to reign in his temper, and glanced at Jonathan, over his shoulder.

"What happened to her?"

Jonathan climbed awkwardly to his feet. "It was her brother, Donnall Maxwell."

Like a wildcat scenting prey, Michael's nostrils flared. "Why?"

The question was not directed at me, so I decided it would be best for me not to answer it. I wasn't sure I'd be able to get my voice to work, anyway.

There was a tense silence, then Jonathan threw up his hands and blurted out, "He thought Alena was hiding you. He thinks you killed his father."

"Donnall thinks I did *what?*" Michael demanded, looking utterly astonished.

Jonathan eyed Michael askance. "His father. Innes Maxwell. You... uh... When you were— That is, they think it was you who, um..."

Jonathan moistened his lips, and averted his eyes. "He's dead, Michael," he finished softly.

Michael's expression warped from astonishment to horrified understanding in a matter of seconds. The grip on my wrists slowly relaxed.

"No," he whispered, shaking his head. *"Not Innes."*

He stared down at my face, silently pleading with me to declare his uncle a liar. I opened my mouth to confirm that what Jonathan had said was true, then realized I had no actual proof that Michael had done it.

A *beast* killed Innes.

Not a man.

But survival was the natural law of the forest. When I looked at Michael, it was all too easy to believe that he was that beast, somewhere inside. All too easy to imagine that sometimes the animal broke through his rigid control and did things the man would never dream of doing. Actions borne from instinct, rather than reason, driven by a mindless urge for self—preservation.

Like the way you reacted when you wrestled that dagger from Ian's hand, drew it back, and slit an innocent man's throat.

The memory of Ian's murder flashed through my mind, striking like a fissure of lightning through my skull. I saw horrific images, vivid and clear, but it was as though I were watching what had happened from *outside* my body. My legs began to wobble uncontrollably. I didn't *want* to remember. Didn't want it to be real.

With an effort, I thrust the images away, and forced myself to concentrate on Michael's face. He looked not-quite-real in the hazy moonlight. Too intense, too powerful. Otherworldly. A half-grown beard darkened the lower portion of his jaw. Through it, his full lips mouthed words I was unable to hear.

Then, without warning, sound came rushing back and flooded silence, mixing and melting with the roaring in my ears.

"...all right? How badly did he hurt her?"

"I don't know." Jonathan's voice sounded muffled. "Passed out cold on me yesterday, but she seemed fine after that."

I felt like a dispassionate observer watching myself from outside my body. Michael leaned down, picked me up, and cradled me against the hard wall of his chest. I snuggled into his embrace, breathed in the pleasant, musky scent of his skin. My thoughts drifted to the strong, steady rhythm of his heartbeat, and the counter—rhythm of his footsteps through the overgrown forest. I felt safe and secure for the first time since setting out on this journey to rescue Michael.

He had ended up rescuing me, instead.

* ~ * ~ *

Michael argued loudly and vehemently against returning to Ashland, but Jonathan stubbornly refused to acquiesce, insisting he would follow Michael to the fiery pits of hell itself, before abandoning him the travesty the Sacred Order called justice. Michael, with evident reluctance, eventually gave in.

We headed northeast, toward the edge of the Great Shield that protected my homeland from the *advena.* As the evening progressed, conversation gradually changed to mundane but necessary questions such as, *Which direction should we go in? How long will it take to get there?* and *How much water is left in the waterskins?*

Despite the danger dogging our heels, all I could seem to concentrate on was Michael—his gorgeous face and muscular build, the rough sound of his broken voice. Before leaving Jackson's cabin, Jonathan had remembered to bring along Michael's backpack with a spare change of clothing inside, just in case. It was a good thing he did, I remarked privately. With my senses on overload, I wasn't sure how much more of Michael's naked, masculine splendor I would have been able to stand.

Lacking the night vision all descendants of Corvus had been blessed with, Jonathan was having a hard time keeping up with Michael and me. Sometime after midnight, the three of us cleared out a rough circle in the underbrush, then settled down to steal a precious few hours of rest. I lay on my side on a soft bed of leaves. Michael reclined across from me in much the same position, while Jonathan was sprawled horizontally on the ground at our feet, snoring loudly.

Like the echo of a long-standing family quarrel, the word *lifemate* hung in the air between us, but it seemed neither of us was ready to acknowledge it. With a weary sigh, I rolled onto my back. The night sky was crowded with millions of bright stars. Leaves and branches swayed in the breeze, while an owl hooted its melancholy song. The chorus of insects faded into the background of my troubled thoughts, as I tried to make sense of our situation. What offended Corvus, according to the priests, was the perversion of *In Bestiae Corpore Transmuto,* His most sacred of gifts. But Michael's ability to transform was not weakened or corrupted by human blood, therefore it would seem that he was whole in the eyes of the god and did not deserve to be executed.

Michael was something beyond cursed. Not an abomination, but an anomaly. I was afraid, however, that I would be the only one who saw it that way, and I was not in any position to influence Michael's fate.

I felt foolish and awkward. This love business was damned inconvenient. I was drawn to Michael as I'd never been to any other man. Simply being near him made me feel things I'd never felt before. Strange, frightening, alien feelings. But the sole heir to the title of Guardian of the Dead could not choose a man who was cursed to be her *lifemate*. Even if the man in question just happened to be the first male in two hundred years powerful enough to transform.

I turned my head, and our gazes met. The rhythm of his breathing was steady and soothing, and my fingers itched to smooth away the worried frown that creased his brow. Long, black lashes drifted down, masking the turmoil in his midnight eyes.

He reached out, and drew me into his embrace. My heartbeat quickened, and my skin tingled in anticipation. Strong fingers massaged my neck and scalp, combed gently through the tangles in my hair.

"Don't be afraid," he whispered, close to my ear. "It's only me."

At first, I thought it was an odd choice of words. After all, who else would it be? Then I remembered the first night we had spent together. He had used that same phrase several times that night, and I realized it must be Michael's way of letting me know he had the beast under control.

He lowered his head. Sharp teeth nipped softly on my earlobe; his warm breath tickled my neck. He lifted his head, and his full lips lingered just above mine.

"Love me, Alena. *Si placet.* "

Before I could think or react, his lips met mine in a kiss so gentle, so tender, it made me ache with longing. The ground turned to quicksand and tried to swallow me. The world spun dangerously, and I clung to Michael, suddenly wanting — *needing* — his strength to make me feel whole. He sucked in his breath as my hands slipped beneath the shirt to caress his broad shoulders and muscular back. His skin felt smooth and firm, smelled of musk and rain and wet earth. Strong hands explored my body beneath my clothing, wave after wave of blissful sensations trailing in their wake.

He removed my trousers first, then his own, and fitted his hips between my thighs. His rigid member pressed against my center. There was a flash of pain as he entered. I cried out, and the muscles in his arms and shoulders tensed as he held himself perfectly still above me. Tangled black waves fell over his eyes. I reached up, and gently brushed them away.

He moved within me, slowly at first, igniting tiny sparks that flared into flames and spread like wildfire through my every nerve ending.

Gods of earth and sky, how had I lived so long without him?

I remember thinking there must be a terrible price to pay for such ecstasy—then decided that whatever the price, it was worth it.

He cried out his release and collapsed on top of me, panting hard, skin slick with moisture. I massaged the hard muscles of his broad back, listened to the steady *thump thump thump* of his heart beating in time to the music of the forest.

A strong gust of wind invaded our sanctuary, chilled my exposed skin, and rustled through the underbrush, sending dry leaves scattering in all directions.

"Michael," I whispered, after we'd lain for a long time, not moving. "I can't breathe."

Supporting his weight on his elbows, he nuzzled his stubble-covered cheek against mine. I breathed in deeply through my nose, and basked in the afterglow of our joining. A moment later, Michael's lips blazed a warm trail of kisses down my neck and shoulders. His tongue laved my nipples, causing them to ache and harden. My insides clenched, and he groaned in response.

"Hold still, my love, or I will die with pleasure."

Hazy moonlight highlighted the planes and angles of his face, flickering and dancing with the shadows in his eyes. Looking at Michael was akin to watching a colorful sunset over the mountains or the frozen landscape of winter shining in the sun.

Breathtaking. Heart-wrenching. Devastating.

I felt mesmerized by his beauty, captivated by the dark, pulsating energy simmering just below the surface, dizzy with the knowledge that so much power could be mine to command.

A surge of emotion, raw and primitive, compelled me to sink my teeth into the skin of his neck. Warm blood trickled over my lips, and onto my tongue. The taste was rich and intoxicating. I drank of it deeply, then heard, as though from a long ways away, a low voice chanting in the tongue of the ancients.

"Together we are born
Together we die

We walk through the Physical World
Two bodies, one soul
Sealed in Blood.
The law of Corvus is truth
The truth is sacred."

Awareness returned slowly, like retreating fog. I felt a sinking sensation in the pit of my belly. Michael jerked back sharply, as though he'd been struck by an invisible hand, and gaped at me in wordless surprise. Panic flashed in his eyes, then he quickly rolled off me, and sat up. When I moved to do the same, his arm shot out and held me in place.

With one hand planted firmly on my chest, he leaned out, grabbed his discarded shirt and spread it over me like a blanket. Then he shook his tousled mane of black hair, and withdrew to the other side of the tiny clearing. With stiff, jerky movements, he retrieved his trousers and pulled them on.

He stood there for a long time, hands on hips, his back to me. Broad shoulders rose and fell with his rapid breathing, as though he'd traversed miles instead of mere feet.

"You could have at least asked me first," he ground out.

When I didn't reply, he reached down and tossed me my clothing. I managed to dress myself, even though my hands were shaking so much I was barely able to fasten the buttons.

The words I had spoken echoed in my head. The sacred mating spell, the *Prayer Of Bonding*—a spell that would binds us together for the lengths of our lifetimes.

The look in Michael's eyes beneath his lowered brows was full of reproach and laced with betrayal. I didn't blame him for being angry, but there was no good way to explain that I hadn't meant to do it. The spell was cast, and could not be undone.

"I'm sorry," I mumbled weakly. "It was an accident. I was a little overwhelmed by your... uh... I mean, I didn't intend—"

"An *accident?*" A muscle jumped in his cheek, and his nostrils flared with the effort to control his fury. "You bind us together for eternity, and call it an *accident?* What the hell were you thinking, Alena?"

Though I knew I deserved it, I bristled at the scolding. "I said I'm sorry. It's not like I can fix it or anything, so we're just going to have to make the best of it. And anyway, it's not completely my fault. You were the one who wanted—"

"Don't say it," he warned, voice tight with barely—leashed emotion. "Don't you dare turn a beautiful memory into something ugly. You wanted me inside you just as much as I wanted to be there. Don't forget, my love, I can smell your desire."

A blush warmed my cheeks, and my eyes burned with unshed tears. I stared at the ground, determined not to let him see how much his crude words had wounded me.

After a few moments, I heard his footsteps, coming closer. I considered getting up and moving away, but avoiding the problem was only going to make things worse.

But then, why was I thinking of this mating in terms of a mistake that needed to be fixed, rather than what it ought to be—a cause for celebration? Bonding with one's *lifemate* ought to be a joyous occasion. Some people never find their true mates, spend their lives empty and alone, never quite whole. I should feel elated, not remorseful, should be on my knees thanking the gods for my good fortune.

"Alena."

His husky voice floated in the air around my head; its echo, like smoke, trailed in the breeze. I didn't turn around, though I could sense his presence behind me. I felt his gaze on my back like the heat of a too-warm fire.

"We need to talk."

I pressed my lips tightly together, and fought the urge to look over my shoulder. He circled around, and knelt in front of me. I focused on his bare foot resting on the leafy ground, the way his trousers strained across his bent knee, the large veins that stood out on the backs of his hands. He cleared his throat, and exhaled slowly.

"I'm not sure how to explain this so you'll understand. Don't think I would not be honored to spend the rest of my life with you as my mate, Alena. It's just that I'm not exactly sure what I'm capable of. I'm afraid I might... *It* might..."

The rigid muscles of his forearms flexed and contracted as his hands curled into tight fists. "There might still be a way to sever the bond. For your own safety, my love. You must set yourself free."

A surge of anger caused me to leap to my feet. Seething in silence, I looked around wildly for something to use to knock some sense into that gorgeous head of his. Finding nothing immediately to hand but Michael's shirt and my own soft-soled leather boots, I folded my arms across my chest and stalked to the opposite side of the tiny clearing.

We stared at each other over Jonathan's snoring body. Tension, anger, and mutual frustration swirled around us, thick as the fog that crept through the underbrush.

I lifted my chin and glared at him. "I wasn't going to mention this, but I happened to be there the day you killed Innes."

Michael's face drained of color. His lashes flickered, and he averted his eyes.

"I know what you're capable of, Michael. I've seen you at your worst. But I've also seen you control the madness, and I know that you would never let yourself hurt me."

He growled, low in his throat. The sound was deep and menacing. My heart fluttered inside my chest, and I took an involuntary step backward.

He stepped over Jonathan's motionless body and stalked toward me. Strong fingers curled around my upper arms, slid over my elbows, and captured my wrists. The breath caught in my throat as he leaned in. His broken voice crawled over my skin, and burrowed deep, like a swarm of biting insects.

"I don't *want* to hurt you, Alena, but I'll probably do it anyway. It's *his* body, not mine. *Bestiae* doesn't care what Michael wants."

"I'll help you," I whispered, wanting nothing more than to ease the pain I saw in his eyes. "We'll go to the castle and tell my father everything. He'll find a way to get you out of this. According to Sacred Law, the cursed are an affront to Corvus because they're unable to transform. But once the council sees that you *can* transform, they'll have to let you go free."

His gaze searched mine as his calloused palm gently caressed my cheek. "How naive you are, my love. Don't you understand that confessing my secret would only make them more determined to get rid of me?"

"Wh—what do you mean?" I asked, puzzled.

Michael shook his head wearily. "It doesn't matter. I don't want you to worry about me, Alena. I can take care of myself. As soon as it's daylight, I want you to go home, to the castle. I'm going to take my uncle through the Shield, then I'll hide out in the forest until you find a way to break the mating spell."

For some inexplicable reason, the thought of going back to the castle alone terrified me. "I can't go back without you!"

"You have to," he insisted. "I'll be able to feel when the bond has been released. As soon as you're free, I plan to return to the land of the *advena.*"

I frowned in confusion. "But the mating spell is for life. What if there *is* no way to break the bond? Why can't I come with you?"

"There has to be a way," he insisted, ignoring my last question. "All you did was invoke the spell. There was no ceremony performed by a priest. It might not be permanent."

"Michael—" I began, but he cut me off.

"You *have* to do this, Alena. This fight is between the Sacred Order and me, alone. I don't want you involved. I want to make sure you're safe."

For a moment, all I could do was gape at him in incredulous silence.

"Has the fact that I killed Ian MacDonald completely slipped your mind?" I blurted out, my temper rising again. "If I go back, they're most likely going to arrest me. And how do you suggest I go about telling my father that I've taken a man he believes to be cursed as my *lifemate?* I'm already *involved,* Michael."

"The mating is probably only temporary. There's no reason for your father or anyone else to know about it. As for the dead guard, they'll probably blame me for the killing, so there's no need to tell them about that, either. The less they know about us, the better."

"You want me to live a lie? Michael, I don't know if I can do that. And why *should* I do it? They'll only want to help—"

"No!" He gripped my shoulders and shook me, hard. A dangerous glint appeared in his eyes. "If the tribe finds out that you've mated with me, they'll treat you differently. They'll try to use you to get to me."

"But how am I supposed to find a way to break the spell without asking someone?" I protested. "I'm just an acolyte. Only Guardians have access to the scrolls of Sacred Law."

He was silent so long, I was beginning to think he wasn't going to answer. Thick, black lashes veiled his eyes. He cleared his throat, and a muscle jumped inside his cheek.

"Your father is the Guardian of the Dead," he said, finally. "You must know where he keeps the scrolls."

His meaning was clear: break into my father's library, find the scrolls of Sacred Law, and read them for myself. But it was a sin for anyone but a priest to read the sacred scrolls. As the ramifications of what he was suggesting began to sink in, my body began to tremble violently.

I couldn't stop shaking, even when Michael wrapped his arms around me and pulled me into a warm embrace. My face pressed against his bare chest as his hands massaged the back of my neck.

"Just trust me, my love. It's going to be all right."

No, I thought wearily. *It isn't.*

It was beginning to seem as though nothing would ever be all right again.

CHAPTER TEN
Duplicity

Michael Singleton
Blackwater Hills

Michael's spirit detached from his body and rose to hover high in the treetops. He stared down at the world spread out beneath him. Mist and fog carpeted the forest floor and draped over leaves and branches, waving in the gentle breeze like torn spider's webs. The moon's hazy, silverblue light illuminated an animal climbing slowly up the treacherous slope of the mountain.

Michael instantly recognized his bestial form, though he had never before seen his other side. He watched, fascinated, as the creature gained its footing on a flat patch of land, opened its powerful jaws, and howled a mournful cry that echoed through the wilderness.

Every living thing within earshot scrambled for cover, finding safety in underbrush, dens, or tree trunks. After a few moments, the animal lowered its head. Panting, the beast laid down upon a pile of leaves, its bright pink tongue lolling against the backdrop of its thick, black fur.

Bestiae was larger than Michael had imagined when he had tried to picture what his other side might look like. Its limbs appeared sturdier than those of a wolf, but not quite as broad and powerful as a bear's.

Its muzzle was long and pointed, crowded with canines and incisors that made Michael's look like milk teeth in comparison. Its ears brought to mind those of a German Shepherd, and the tail was covered in fur and slightly curved at the end. As to its eyes...

Michael recognized the eyes as his own. Even from far away, the emotions they reflected were unmistakable. They were what he saw every time he gazed into a mirror—confusion, shame, bitterness, fear—which was why he went out of his way to avoid mirrors, glass, still pools of water, or anything reflective. He couldn't stand the sight of his own vulnerability. It made him feel weak and anxious to know that others might be able to see behind the mask. Michael didn't want anyone inside his head—including himself, most of the time.

Without warning, he plummeted to earth. His spirit slammed full force back into his body before his mind had time to register the sensation of falling. But the body he returned to was not that of a beast; it was his man-form in which he found himself. Keeping a wary eye on the creature lying prostrate on the ground a few feet away, he stood up.

Bestiae's lips curled back in a submissive grin, and there was nothing in the animal's body language to indicate a challenge to Michael's dominance. Still, it was the creature's eyes that revealed its true intentions.

Michael began to remove his clothing. His shirt, followed by his scuffed black leather boots and wrinkled trousers, landed in a heap on the forest floor. Slowly, purposefully, he advanced upon his adversary.

The fog seemed to magnify every sound; with every step, the crunch of twigs and dry leaves resonated like shots from a rifle. He stopped mere inches from the animal's long muzzle, and with a pain-filled roar, surrendered to the change.

Two beasts, identical in height and coloring, circled each other like swordsmen engaged in a duel. Growls and snarls swirled round through the fog as each one bared their teeth in warning. Neither beast took heed, and the battle commenced. The world became fur and fangs and blood, growls and snarls and yelps of pain, the rabid desire to drain an enemy's life-force.

But they were too well matched. It soon became obvious that neither would prevail in the contest for dominance, and both animals collapsed upon the ground, panting heavily.

The beast that was Michael raised its head. He saw his rival begin to change seconds before feeling the pain of his own transformation. His man-form was covered in bruises and sticky patches of blood, but most of the wounds had already begun to heal. Michael grabbed hold of a low-hanging branch and pulled himself up. Through half-closed eyelids, he regarded the man-form of his adversary.

Michael felt the limb bow dangerously beneath his weight, gripped it with both hands, and fought to stay upright. Rough bark dug into his calloused palms. The world swam in and out of focus. Panic swept through him. He could taste it, like bile, in the back of his throat.

"You are not..." He choked out. "You are not... Michael."

The Other walked slowly toward him. Moonlight outlined the muscular contours of his body, and glittered in his midnight eyes as he glared accusingly at Michael.

"They punished her, instead of you. You stood by and did nothing, watched us suffer for crimes you committed."

Michael shook his head. The world spun dangerously, then righted itself. "I don't know what you're talking about. Who are you?"

The Other stopped mere inches from his face. They stared at each other for the space of a heartbeat. Hatred blazed in the eyes of his rival.

"My name is Samuel," rasped the Other. "They call me the Merula. I am not you, I am your tainted legacy—the weapon used to destroy the only woman who ever loved you."

The fiercely uttered words were Michael's undoing. Darkness seeped around the edges of his vision. The branch slipped from his grasp, and he felt himself falling.

The Other reached out, grabbed Michael's shoulders with both hands, and shoved him hard against the trunk of the tree.

"Now I am going to destroy you, so the Balance will be restored."

"No," Michael protested weakly. He could do no more than that. His eyelids drifted shut against his will. His limbs seemed suddenly made of lead, his thoughts slow and ponderous.

Am I dying, he wondered? It did not seem like such a bad thing, if so.

"Michael!"

He opened his eyes. Slowly, the face of the Other disintegrated, and was replaced with...

Alena.

"Michael, *wake up!"*

His heart thundered inside his chest. He bent over, fighting to hold down the meager contents of his stomach. Alena laid a hand on his shoulder, and he jerked away. Close as she was, she overwhelmed his senses. He needed a moment to regain his composure. On hands and knees, he crawled to the nearest tree and leaned against it, panting like he'd run for miles through the wilderness. The harsh, rasping voice of the Other echoed in his head.

The weapon used to destroy the only woman who ever loved you.

Michael's gaze flew to Alena's stomach, hidden in the baggy folds of her oversize flannel shirt. A wave of dread washed over him as he realized what he'd done. He swallowed around a thick lump in his throat.

"What's wrong?" A tiny frown creased the creamy smoothness of her forehead.

"Nothing," he said, quickly.

Alena's frown deepened. "Did you have a bad dream?"

It's possible she's not *pregnant,* the voice of Logic (which sounded suspiciously like Jonathan) spoke up inside his head. *You only made love once, you know.*

Once is all it takes, replied the voice of Instinct. And as much as Michael respected the opinion of his uncle, it was the latter voice he was more inclined to listen to.

"You were talking in your sleep," Alena informed him. "Yelling, actually."

Her eyes narrowed suspiciously. He imagined he looked like some wild creature, half out of his mind with terror. He took a deep breath, and tried his best to crush the residual fear that hummed like a motor through his every nerve ending.

It was just a stupid dream, Logic insisted. *Get a grip, Michael.*

"Do you want to tell me about it?"

He shook his head.

She breathed a long-suffering sigh, reached over, and retrieved her backpack. "Are you hungry?" She asked, rifling through the sack of leftover food.

"Thirsty," he said, wincing at the way his voice scraped the inside of his throat, rough like sandpaper.

She stood up and handed him the half-empty waterskin. He breathed in the lingering scent of lovemaking that clung to her skin, and wondered— not for the first time—why she had come looking for him.

The transformation had broken the spell he had cast to probe her mind, and Michael wasn't sure he believed in soul mates—or *lifemates,* as his people called them. The notion that he was half a soul and would not feel complete until he found his other side, seemed like little more than romantic fallacy. It was a nice idea, but like most things of that nature, it was probably too good to be true.

Besides, he had more *other sides* than he could handle at the moment. As much as he desired Alena, he could not drag her into the mess that was his life, could not expect her to want to stay with him. She deserved better, someone who could provide her with a home and children, someone who would take care of her and keep her safe, a man she didn't have to fear when the moon was full.

Not someone like him, who wasn't really a man at all.

"Michael? Are you sure you're all right?'"

He met her eyes briefly, then glanced away. He cleared his throat, then stood up on shaking legs. A light breeze rustled through the branches overhead. Michael leaned against a tree, closed his eyes, and inhaled the damp, rich smell of approaching dawn.

Every new day is a new beginning, Aunt Stella used to say. *Another chance to let go of the past.*

There was much in Stella's past she would have liked to break free of, but Michael suspected she was never quite able to completely forget. The mind held on, even to its detriment, like a starving dog gnawing on a pile of ancient bones.

The past—and now, the future—haunted Michael, as well.

As for the present...

"Should we wake Jonathan?" Alena asked softly from behind him.

Her voice sounded resigned, but apprehensive, as though she too feared the reality awaiting them outside the protection of their tiny clearing.

"Let him sleep a bit yet," he answered, even though he knew they didn't have much time.

Michael wasn't sure exactly how the Sacred Order would punish the daughter of the Guardian of the Dead, but he had a damn good idea what his own fate was likely to be. It was best that he not be anywhere near Alena if—or, rather, *when*—the guards found him.

Aside from the chance that the guards might discover their hiding place, there was another looming threat: it wouldn't be long before the onset of another episode.

The full moon was weeks away. The risk of a full transformation was not an issue at the moment, but the longer they were together, the more likely it was to happen in front of Alena. He didn't know why his insides curdled at the memory of her seeing him at the mercy of the creature who shared his body. He only knew he didn't want her to witness his weakness, his shame, a second time.

He began gathering up their belongings, what little there was. As he donned his shirt, he slanted a glance at Alena. She was sitting on the ground a few feet away, pointed chin resting on her drawn up knees. He bent down, tapped Jonathan on the shoulder.

"Jay," he called softly. "Time to wake up."

Jonathan mumbled something unintelligible, then rolled over. There were bits of dried leaves in his hair. Thick stubble, peppered with flecks of gray, covered his jaw and upper lip. His bright blue eyes pierced Michael soul, and Michael felt the tiny hairs on the back of his neck prickle with warning.

Then Jonathan blinked, and the sensation vanished. Michael reached out a hand to help his uncle to his feet.

Jonathan waved away Michael's offer of assistance, and with a grunt of effort, pushed himself up from the ground. Alena walked over and stood beside them.

"I guess this is goodbye," she muttered, looking nonplused at the prospect of returning to the castle alone.

"About fucking time," Jonathan muttered under his breath. With a nod to Alena, he grabbed his backpack and strode briskly away, toward the edge of the clearing. "Thanks for all your help, Miss Andrick."

When Michael did not immediately follow, Jonathan stopped and looked over his shoulder.

"Come on, Michael. What the hell are you waiting for? Get us back to civilization!"

CHAPTER ELEVEN
Dark Blue Mind

Alena Andrick
Blackwater Hills

Feeling betrayed and hopeless, I travelled alone through the murky forest, toward the castle. My only consolation was Michael's promise to wait inside the shield while I searched my father's library, but the promise gave me little comfort. If, by some miracle, I did happen to discover a way to break the mating spell, he would then immediately leave Blackwater Hills—and me—forever. The thought of never seeing him again filled me with a terrible sadness. I had never known a man who could make me feel the things Michael Singleton made me feel, and something told me that I never would again.

Though I knew it was selfish, maybe even foolish, I didn't want Michael to go back to the land of the *advena* without me. Despite his protestations to the contrary, I still believed there was a chance we could persuade the Sacred Order to let him live. I wanted him to stay and be my *lifemate,* for I knew down to the marrow of my bones that if I severed the bond now, I'd end up childless and alone until the day I died.

And if the opposite happened, and I was unable to break the spell that bound our souls for eternity? I was forced to admit, that scenario offered even less hope of happily-ever-after. I had personally never known anyone who suffered from the separation sickness common among *lifemates,* but that was only because all the couples I knew who had joined in the sacred mating ceremony had never strayed very far from each other afterwards.

Like all children of the tribe, I'd sat round the bonfire and listened to the stories. It was how the tales were passed down, one generation to another. A fair number of those tales involved *lifemates* who had somehow become separated, either by choice or unfortunate happenstance. The result, in every instance, was tragic.

Don't think about that now, I told myself. What I had to do now, was figure out a way to break the mating spell. If I could not, I would likely end up the pitiful heroine in one of those tales. As I neared the castle, however, I began to seriously question my plan to break into Father's library.

For one thing, I had no idea where my father was at the moment, and didn't want to be caught snooping inside his private domain. For another, the majority of the texts had been written in the Tongue of the Ancients. I'd been taught to read and speak the language, as was every child of Corvus, but it was slow-going and tedious. I didn't have time to waste.

Further, not all of the documents in the vault belonged to Sacred Law. Aside from the obvious—books and papers brought here from the land of the *advena*—I had no way of knowing what belonged and what didn't, unless I scanned through every scroll, parchment, and scrap of paper in the library. I might end up searching for weeks, and never find a scroll that addressed my and Michael's particular problem, much less one that offered a viable solution to it.

I considered my earlier plan to ask Tarren Campbell for help. Elise's *lifemate* was thoughtful, fair, and open-minded, but he was also a priest. His loyalty was pledged to the Sacred Order.

As I tried to decide what to do, the wind whipped my hair in all directions. Lightning flashed above the spiky silhouette of mountains in the distance, and was followed by the warning growl of approaching thunder. Cold droplets of rain stung my exposed skin. I might be able to make it to Tarren and Elise's cabin by mid-afternoon, I thought, with a wary glance toward the sky. If Tarren was willing to offer his help, Michael could be on his way back to the land of the *advena* by nightfall.

Scattered throughout the forest I called home, were cabins in which dwelled the children of Corvus. They had been erected as needed, with no particular pattern in mind, then connected by narrow trails woven through the forest like an intricate spider's web. Some cabins were built of wood, others out of stone, and each was unique to those who had constructed it. Some cabins were large, to accommodate extended families, while others had only one or two rooms. Elise and Tarren Campbell's cabin was in the latter category, resting at the foot of a hill, at the end of a grassy meadow.

When I reached the edge of the forest that surrounded the meadow, I hesitated. To my right, lay the remains of a fallen ash tree, its broken body mostly covered by vines and leaves. I brushed a pile of leaves aside, and sat down. I had to come up with something to say to Tarren, some way to try and persuade him to help Michael avoid the death penalty.

There might be guards patrolling the edge of the forest on the opposite side, I thought. But if someone did spot me crossing the meadow to Elise's cabin, did they even have the right to stop and detain me? I realized that I didn't know, wasn't sure if anyone suspected that my absence the last several days had anything to do with Michael. My half-brother might have, but for all anyone else knew, I could have been camping in the woods, nursing my bruises and my pride after the altercation I'd had with Donnall. It wouldn't have been the first time I'd hid in the woods until my brother's temper had a chance to cool.

That's what I'll say, if anyone asks where I've been. It will buy me some time to come up with a better plan to get Michael out of trouble.

Twilight tiptoed through the forest. Soluna gazed over the mountains, its eye partly obscured by wispy clouds. What few stars were visible looked too tired to sparkle, like they had used every ounce of their energy simply to appear.

Smoke curled out of the cabin's chimney and blended with the hazy, silver sky. Candlelight spilled from two square windows on either side of the front door. A rocking chair creaked on the weathered boards of the front porch, as though the wind had decided to sit down and while away the evening.

Sounds were amplified by the open space of the meadow. From the small barn on the opposite side of the cabin, goats bleated and pigs snorted roughly in answer. Chickens fluttered their wings against the sides of their pens. I heard, in the distance, the rush of the Blackwater River. It sounded—as though, sensing something was amiss—the fresh mountain water was in a hurry to pass through the Blackwater forest.

What am I doing? I asked myself. My chest felt tight, and my muscles tensed with anxiety. I wanted to save Michael, my *lifemate.* Nothing else seemed important. This compulsion—it had driven me to shield Michael during the feast of the *Vernus,* compelled me to search the sacred burial chamber beneath the castle, led me first to Michael's cabin to find him, then here to elicit the help of a Guardian I called friend—was something I could not explain. But it was real. It was powerful. I couldn't seem to control it or make it go away.

Stay far away from the abomination, my father had warned me. Had it been only days ago? So much had happened since, it seemed that it should have taken longer. *Resist the spell that he has put you under. Do not speak his name. Do not conjure him with your mind.*

Claudius Andrick's lilting voice drifted through my thoughts like the whisper of the wind. But I hadn't the faintest idea what *Do not conjure him with your mind* meant. Did it mean that I shouldn't think of Michael at all—as if the mere act of recalling his image somehow strengthened the spell that my father thought Michael had cast on me? A spell, by the way, that I did not believe existed to begin with. I may not have been a Guardian yet, but I was still a child of Corvus. The ancient blood still pulsed in my veins. At the very least, I figured I ought to know if someone had cast a spell on me.

Besides, Michael could do better than to waste his compulsions on me. Mine was probably the last opinion the Sacred Order would consider when making decisions.

But all this speculation was pointless. I was wasting valuable time on useless rumination. I stood up, slung the backpack over my shoulder, and started walking across the meadow.

Nourished by spring rains, tall grasses swished against the legs of my trousers. Crickets and locusts had begun to serenade the night. The music bounced off the edge of the mountains and hung, suspended, above the meadow, like a lure to tempt me back into the safety of the trees.

* ~ * ~ *

"Where did you get this?"

Tarren's face had gone ghostly. Light from the beeswax candle in the center of the table deepened the shadows beneath his eyes, and highlighted the faint creases on either side of his mouth. My hands started sweating. I snatched them off the table, and wrapped them in the trailing hem of my flannel shirt.

"From the sacred burial chamber," I answered, a little shakily.

Tarren sighed, and ran his fingers through his sandy-blond hair. "You're not a Guardian, Alena. You shouldn't go in there."

"It's not forbidden," I said, defensively.

"It isn't," he agreed. "But—" He stopped, shook his head, and seemed to be at a loss for words.

Elise leaned over the table, dark hair cascading over one shoulder, and examined the skull without touching it.

"What's wrong with its teeth?" she asked, sending a puzzled frown in my direction.

"This is a matter for the Sacred Order to handle," Tarren answered before I could say anything. "Neither you nor Alena are members of the Sacred Order, so I'm sorry, but I can't answer those questions."

Elise narrowed her eyes at her *lifemate.* "Oh, come on, Tarren. I'm sure you can tell her something. Who's going to know?"

Tarren stared down at the table, absently tracing the pattern of wood grain with the calloused tip of his index finger. His fingers were stained with dirt from tilling the garden. There was a cut on his thumb, just below the knuckle, and a chunk of nail was missing on his pinkie.

"Why did you bring this to me?" he asked.

I untangled my hands from my shirt, bit my lip, and stared at the skull. Thin wires had been wrapped around the jaws on either side, which held them together as muscle and sinew were boiled away during the cleansing ceremony. The surface looked smooth and dry, the bone discolored with age.

I took a deep breath, and let it out slowly. "I used to play in the tomb when I was little. Father never knew. At least, I don't think he did. I remembered seeing... I mean, when I saw Michael, I remembered that some of the skulls in the tomb had the same... deformity."

I wasn't explaining this very well at all. I thought I knew what I wanted to say, but the words seemed to be floating, just out of reach. My voice echoed in my head, sounding weak and thready. The skull blurred before my eyes, and I blinked rapidly to clear my vision.

Elise's delicate eyebrows shot straight to her hairline. "Are you saying Michael's teeth are like *this?*"

"Yes," I whispered. "He uses a shield to hide them."

Tarren stood up, and began pacing beside the table. The wooden floorboards creaked in protest. "Alena, you mustn't say such things. That cannot have been what you saw. It's impossible."

"Why do you say it's impossible when," I gestured to the skull, "this man clearly had the same issue. It's real, Tarren, whether you want to believe it or not. Is there a way to know whose skull it is? Maybe the man is related to Michael."

Tarren balled his hands into fists, and thrust them into the pockets of his trousers. "There's probably no way to know for certain. Your father is the only Guardian permitted access to the Book of the Dead. As far as I'm aware, the Guardian of the Dead records the names of the deceased who are buried in the tomb, but doesn't keep track of the skull's exact location."

He fixed me with a censorious glare. "Which is fortunate for you, Alena. How many skulls did you displace, looking for this one?"

A flush warmed my cheeks, and I looked away. "They didn't seem to be grouped in any kind of order. I was afraid no one would believe me, unless I had proof."

The ensuing silence stretched so long, it seemed to have a sound all its own. Feeling suddenly weary, I closed my eyes as a wave of nausea coiled through my insides.

Elise's soft, slightly husky voice broke the silence, tethering me back to reality. "If it's true that Michael has this... *deformity*, as Alena put it, then it should be easy enough to verify—shield or no shield."

"It should," agreed Tarren. "But in order to do so, we would have to know where Michael Singleton is. You wouldn't happen to know that?" He stared pointedly at me. "Would you?"

I bit my lip, and shook my head.

Tarren sighed. "Well, this changes everything. *If* it's true."

This last pricked my temper, temporarily banishing the fog from my brain. "Are you calling me a liar?" I demanded. *"Gods of earth and sky,* why would I lie about something like this? It's not as though telling everyone that Michael has teeth like a wolf, is going to help convince the Sacred Order that he doesn't suffer from the blood madness! Think about it, Tarren. How do you suppose they got that way?"

"How, in the name of Corvus, should I know?" he exploded, managing to sound confused, angry, and nervous all at once.

"Look, Alena, I want to help you. But I can't make assumptions without knowing all the facts. The accused has the right to a trial before execution, but make no mistake: the verdict will be the death penalty."

"Yes, but if…" Elise stared to ask something, but he cut her off.

"I am a priest. I have a duty to uphold Sacred Law. I've never seen anything like this before, but it doesn't matter what I think, anyway."

Elise circled the table, and rested a hand on his shoulder. "It might," she said. "What do you think, Tarren?"

He turned to me, his expression stern and serious, matching his voice. "I think," he said carefully, "that you should forget you ever met Michael Singleton. Stay holed up in the castle until his trial and execution are over. Have faith that we in the Sacred Order do what we do for the good of the tribe. Trust us, Alena. Heed your father's warning. Do not conjure him with your mind."

Those words again. I thought of asking Tarren what they meant, but couldn't speak around the lump in my throat. His words were like a punch in the gut. My eyes burned with unshed tears, and I felt like an idiot. Of course, my father had been one step ahead of me. By this time, Father had probably convinced every priest in the Sacred Order that Michael had cast some kind of spell on me. Coming here for help had only made things worse. Now, Tarren would go and tell my father everything.

I turned my head and gazed out the window. Through delicate lace curtains, the night sky was visible. Soluna, ever faithful, watched over the creatures of the night. Tempus marched on with single—minded purpose, while Fatum guarded well His secrets. Venefica plotted revenge upon those She believed had wronged Her, while Corvus remained indifferent to the needs of His children – particularly those who were most like Him. I had yet to find a way to break the mating spell, so Michael would be free to return to the land of the *advena*. I had also ruined any chance of getting Tarren to take up Michael's cause.

All things considered, it had been a most unproductive day.

The realization that I was powerless to influence the outcome of Michael's trial, left a bitter taste in my mouth. I found it difficult to understand such blind allegiance to Sacred Law, but then I was not yet a Guardian. No one cared what I thought, and why should they?

Feeling defeated, I stood up and reached for the skull. As I tucked it inside my backpack, Elise looked over, a question in her eyes.

Are you okay? She mouthed silently.

I answered with a shrug, slung the strap of the pack over my shoulder, and headed for the front door. As I reached for the latch, I heard Elise whispering something to her *lifemate,* but I couldn't dredge up the energy to care what it was. I felt emotionally drained, dizzy, and confused. Rusted hinges creaked as the door swung open. I closed it behind me, and stepped out into the night.

* ～ * ～ *

An acolyte was given twelve chances to pass the initiation to become a full-fledged member of the Sacred Order. Most—like Donnall—gave up after chance three or four, but some—like Tarren

Campbell—had stuck it out and managed to pass the initiation on the final try.

I had not yet finished my schooling, which generally took about five years to complete. I was only halfway through year three, and would not be eligible to be put through the series of tests until *Brumalis,* the Winter Solstice on the twenty-first of December—next year.

It was possible that what it means to conjure someone with your mind, had not yet been explained in any of my courses. Surely, I thought, I would have remembered. As I traveled through the forest toward the castle, I searched my store of knowledge, but came up with nothing that seemed to fit.

Just a few miles south of the castle, was the meeting place of the Sacred Order. We affectionately called it Mystery Hill, for the enigmatic magic in the ancient standing stones could not be denied. It was not a place for quiet reflection or contemplative prayer, however. The Sanctuary in the castle basement was better suited to that. The energy emitting from the ground on Mystery Hill was intense, and sometimes violent in the way it could seize upon one's soul—forcing it to acknowledge truths that were destructive and painful. It was for that reason, acolytes were never allowed to perform rituals among the standing stones. The risk of inadvertently unleashing something terrible was too great.

Mystery Hill was also the place where the Ritual of Execution was performed after an Evaluation. Evaluations were done upon the giant stone slab that served as an altar, and also in the large stone chamber directly below it. An Evaluation followed a strict set of procedures dictated by Sacred Law. We had been taught that the ritual had been given to us by the god, Corvus, to prove beyond a shadow of a doubt whether a man was cursed with the blood madness.

The Beast God was angered by our failure to keep His blood pure. By thinning our blood with the blood of the *advena,* we had weakened the gifts He had so lovingly bestowed upon us. It was said that no male could yet be born to the tribe who was pure enough to achieve transformation, and so we must atone for our sins and purge the corrupted males.

These truths were the foundation of Sacred Law. They were things I had always know, always believed. I had spent the last three and a half years training to uphold the laws of my people. It was something I was passionate about, something that— on some level—defined who I was. But all of that changed the day I met Michael Singleton.

My *lifemate.*

Do not conjure him with your mind.

Not wanting to cross through the vortex of Mystery Hill, I veered around it, through the woods, and planned to backtrack toward the castle. But with only a short distance to go, I stopped to wonder if going back to the castle would be my best option. I had already decided that there was no way I would be able to break into my father's library and search through the scrolls. I had planned to ask Tarren if he knew of a way to break the mating spell, but then lost my nerve, and decided not to tell him or Elise that Michael and I had invoked the spell. Donnall could be there, as well, lying in wait for me, believing that I would be able to lead him to Michael.

I cleared out a little circle in the underbrush, sat down, and pulled the waterskin from my backpack.

My stomach rumbled, and I realized I hadn't eaten since breakfast. As I felt around in my pack for the last bits of dried meat and cheese, a loud, male voice boomed through the moonlit forest.

"Cessio! By order of the Guard!"

Corvus have mercy.

Donnall had found me.

He closed the short distance between us, and within seconds, his forearm curled around my neck like an iron vise. I coughed and wheezed, bucking wildly against the brick wall of his body.

In a series of quick and practiced movements, his other hand took possession of both my wrists and jerked them up sharply behind my back. Rough bark scraped my face as he spun me around and slammed me against a tree.

"Wh—what do you want?" I blurted on a rush of pent-up breath.

"Don't test my patience, sister," he snarled as I whimpered in pain. "I know you were with him. His scent is all over you."

I tried to pull away, but he tightened his iron grip on my wrists. I was ill-equipped to win a physical contest with my half-brother, and fear had scattered my wits—the only weapon I possessed. My mind went blank the instant I tried to formulate a lie that might convince Donnall to let me go.

The sound of my breathing was harsh and loud. Sweat trickled down my armpits, despite the chill in the air. The sharp scent of mint pierced my nostrils, and the dull pain of a headache throbbed behind my eyes.

Donnall jerked me around, and propelled me away from the castle, back the way I had come. When

I struggled, his response was to haul me up and carry me as though I were little more than a defiant toddler. I kicked and thrashed, leaning forward to try and throw him off balance. My heel connected with his shin, and I heard his low grunt of pain.

"I'll chain you, if you force me to it," he warned, voice low and menacing. "Be still."

"You'll never get away with this," I spat, though the tremor in my voice betrayed my uncertainty.

"Who's going to stop me?" He sneered.

It was obviously a rhetorical question, for it was painfully clear that *I* couldn't, and there was no one else around to do it.

For the first time in my life, I was genuinely afraid of my half-brother. We had always been rivals; this wasn't the first time one of our confrontations had turned physical. But somehow, I sensed that this time was different. I had always taken for granted that Donnall would exercise some restraint, that he would never cross that invisible line and cause me serious harm.

Now, I was forced to wonder how far he would go to avenge his father. Innes Maxwell had ruled his son with an iron fist. Everyone knew Donnall deeply resented his father's domineering ways. Some young men might have cloaked such bitterness in stoic silence. Donnall was the opposite, and tended toward obnoxious and violent behavior. I never doubted that all he had ever wanted was Innes's approval, however. And now Michael had robbed Donnall of the chance—slim, though it may have been—that he might someday be deemed worthy of his father's love and acceptance.

This realization took root and sprouted; its fruit was the certainty that the need to avenge his father's death had carried Donnall across that imaginary line. He was in no mood to listen to reason, and would never believe the truth, which was that I had no idea where Michael was and did not have the faintest clue how to go about finding him. I was starting to think that my brother might actually kill me, if I did not cooperate.

Thorny vines snatched at my clothes and hair, scraping the skin on my hands and forearms. Thunder rumbled in the sky overhead. The storm had held off all day, but now it threatened to unleash its pent-up fury.

It wasn't long before we reached a narrow section of the Blackwater River, over which a makeshift bridge had been erected. Less than a hundred yards from the bridge, we were met by Seamus MacDonald running on the path in the opposite direction. He nearly crashed into me head on, but at the last second Donnall spun us around, absorbing the impact with his right shoulder.

Seamus stumbled backwards and doubled over, hands on his knees, air wheezing in and out of his lungs. "Donnall," he panted. "Where've you been? I've been looking for you for three days."

"Out hunting," Donnall said curtly.

"You ain't gonna believe it, man. Ian's dead!"

Donnall stiffened. His hand tightened painfully around my captured wrists. "What happened?" he demanded.

"We found his body, day before yesterday. Over by the river, not too far from that old broken down cabin. His throat had been cut with his own knife!"

Donnall swore viciously. Seamus narrowed his eyes and peered through the gloom, as though noticing me for the first time.

He shot a puzzled glance at Donnall. "What'd ya bring her for?"

"She was with him."

Tension radiated from Donnall's body like heat from a bonfire. He whirled around, gripped my shoulders, and shoved me against the nearest tree. I grunted, more from surprise than actual pain. He reached for his belt, and unhooked a length of sturdy rope, secured my wrists together behind the tree, then stepped back, running his fingers through his shaggy brown hair.

With a frustrated growl, he spun on his heel and began to pace back and forth along the narrow path. Seamus, a deep frown etched in the center of his dirt-streaked forehead, hurriedly stepped out of the way.

"She was with him," Donnall repeated, his voice low and dangerous. *"Traitorous bitch."*

Endless, tension-filled moments passed. Seamus's frown deepened, crinkling the weathered skin around his beady eyes. He opened his mouth to say something, but nothing emerged. The blood froze in my veins, as my half-brother lifted his head and pierced my soul with his icy, green gaze.

"It was *you,"* he accused in a deadly whisper. "You killed Ian to protect the abomination, didn't you?"

Panic rose within me, making it suddenly difficult to draw air into my lungs.

A slow smile spread across his face, twisting his handsome features into a grotesque and menacing mask.

"Don't look so shocked, little sister," he murmured, the words dripping with hatred and deadly promise. "I know you've always underestimated me. But you're not as smart as you think you are. Mark my words: before the next day is done, you will pay for your crimes and know the heartache that is felt by our mother. You'll know exactly how it feels when your *lifemate* is murdered."

Donnall turned to Seamus. "Keep an eye on her," he ordered. "I'll be right back."

Seamus glanced from me to Donnall, then nodded uncertainly. Donnall stalked down the path, his tall form blending with the shadows of approaching dawn. A clap of thunder sounded overhead, and I jerked against my bonds, desperate to free myself before he returned.

Seamus chuckled wickedly, apparently amused by my impotent struggle. I looked up, searching his face through the shadows, hoping against hope that I might arouse his sympathy. I'd known Seamus MacDonald all my life. He was family of a sort— brother to Donnall's lifemate, Shaina. He wouldn't just stand by and watch Donnall carry out whatever diabolical plan he had in store for me.

Would he?

Then all hope burned to cinders when I realized what I'd done. The taste of its death was like ashes, and the embers burned all the way down to my soul. Feeling utterly defeated, I ceased my useless fight against the ropes, and lowered my head to avoid Seamus's eyes and the bitter truth I saw reflected there.

Ian MacDonald was Seamus's only brother. I owed him a blood debt for taking Ian's life, and if the expression in Seamus's eyes was any indication, he was prepared to do anything in his power to ensure that it was paid.

Donnall returned about an hour later. He carried an armload of heavy iron chains, with a bulging pack slung over one shoulder. By that time, the clouds had rolled over the mountains, carrying with them the threat of rain. He loosened the rope from the tree, but did not untie my wrists. With the long end of the rope wrapped tightly around one hand, my brother spun me around and shoved me ahead of him.

"Let's go."

With my hands securely tied behind my back, I stumbled ahead of Donnall. Seamus muttered a curse, then I heard his footsteps behind us.

I twisted halfway around to look at them. "What are you going to do to me?" My voice trembled with the uncanny certainty that I really didn't want to know.

"The question is not what *I* am going to do, little sister," he replied, twisting his lips into an expression meant to be a smile, but more resembling a sneer of contempt. "Instead, you should ask yourself how far you are willing to fall to protect an abomination."

I didn't have to ask, for I already knew; I would do whatever it took to keep Michael safe. Though the impulse to protect my *lifemate* was, at its core, born of selfishness—not heroism. I simply did not want to live without Michael, and if that meant fighting against the Guard, the Sacred Order, and Sacred Law, I was prepared to do just that.

"I can't lead you to Michael," I bit out. "I don't know where he is. For all I know, he's already on his way back to the land of the *advena.*"

"If he's still inside the Great Shield, you can and will find him, Alena. Not only will you locate him, you will compel him to come to you."

"How do you expect me to do that?" I retorted, and was honestly surprised when my half-brother provided a means I hadn't even considered.

"I may not be a priest, but I know that *Animus Rimor* can be second-nature between *lifemates*. Do you take me for a fool?"

I was obliged to abandon the mystery of how Donnall had managed to figure out that Michael and I had joined in the sacred mating ceremony—and also that I was the one responsible for the death of Ian MacDonald—when it became clear that Donnall intended to force me to become an unwilling participant in the death of my own *lifemate.*

I could think of no way to get out of doing what he wanted. Michael had lost control and killed Innes Maxwell. Now Donnall was going to claim his due. *In Vindicare.* It was our way, and my brother was operating well within the law. That I was being used as a pawn in Donnall's game of revenge was the ultimate irony.

I could have refused to do what he ordered, but at what cost? Seamus was now aware that I had killed his brother. I chose to believe I had done it in self-defense, but I couldn't prove it. Seamus might very well decide to claim his own vengeance, if I refused to locate Michael.

Corvus save us, I prayed. *For you're the only one who can.*

* ~ * ~ *

How well is it possible to know someone else? Can we look inside another person's soul, hear their thoughts, and feel their feelings? If it were somehow possible, would it draw us closer? Or would it only serve to drive us further apart?

I found the answers to those questions in his dark blue mind. I discovered something about my own self, in the process: I was better off not knowing, better off not having touched the darkness that lived inside him, infinitely better off never having met the mind of the man destined to be my *lifemate.*

But once I began, there was no turning back.

The priests say every person's spirit has a unique color that is invisible to the untrained eye, but detectable by those blessed with the powers of a Guardian. An aura is never static, shifting and evolving along with a person's mood, life experiences, or state of mind. There are no purely good or purely evil colors, for color itself exits in a perfectly balanced state. There are, however, dark and light—reflections of the Bright Star filtered through unique lines of energy.

Sitting in a classroom listening to Simon Kendrick lecture on the subject of auras, however, did not in any way prepare me for the experience of feeling one. It was as though Michael's aura was truly alive, a writhing, pulsing, indigo mass, a giant snake trying to devour me.

And there was *music!* A wonder I had never before experienced. Music was forbidden to the children of Corvus, for it had been invented by His sister, the witch. The Witch had used the sounds as weapons to control her brother, for music and the plant wolfsbane were his only weaknesses.

It was a gloriously seductive sound. I wanted to surrender, lose myself inside it forever. Once I'd heard it, it was as though my soul was starving for melody, and would give almost anything to never be without it again.

Then the music faded, and was replaced with the rhythm of the spoken word, a sound every bit as melodic and beautiful, but one that transported me to an entirely different plane. The words had deep meaning to Michael, and he repeated them often, like a chant or a prayer. As he did so, he struggled to claw his way out of the abyss that threatened to consume his soul.

Every night and every morn
Some to misery are born
Every morn and every night
Some are born to sweet delight
Some are born to sweet delight
Some are born to endless night.

I recognized the poem, for every child of the tribe was expected to study the written works and history of the *advena.* We were outnumbered by them, dependent on their goodwill and indifference in order to survive. *Know thy lot, know thine enemies, and know thyself,* as Mother would say.

It was important that humans not learn too much of our ways, or even believe we existed at all. Being relegated to mythical creatures did not bother us in the least. We would gladly take our places beside witches, vampires, faeries, and *daemons* if it meant our people would be left alone to worship Corvus in peace.

Until I had been inside Michael's mind, I had never understood that for those suffering from the blood madness, life was a never-ending war for dominance between man and beast. A cursed man's soul was a battleground, a house divided. A Guardian was needed to help him tip the scales in his favor, but Michael had none. That he had lasted this long without one, was due to his incredible strength of will, his iron resolve, and his ability to ascend to the Balance on his own. Such a feat was most assuredly the exception that proved the rule, however, and even Michael's iron will was not infallible.

"Is he still inside the Great Shield?" Donnall asked, his voice sounding hollow and faraway.

"Yes," I answered.

"Compel him to come to you," he ordered.

On some level, I was aware of the vines and branches brushing against my trousers and Donnall's firm hand curled around my upper arm, propelling me onward. Each step brought Michael closer to danger, and every fiber of my being screamed out a desperate warning — one he was unable to hear, though I couldn't seem to understand why he couldn't hear me, didn't *know* me, the same way I knew him.

How could he not feel me inside his head?

Michael's soul was laid bare to my eyes, every memory, every thought accessible to me, had I the time or inclination to hear each one and digest its meaning. Donnall had forced me to perform the spell called *Animus Rimor,* more commonly translated as *exploring another's mind.* The spell was one I had never practiced, one I had not yet learned in any of my courses. I had known that it was possible to pick up bits and pieces of another's thoughts or feelings, but what I was doing—the intensity of what I was *feeling*—had taken me completely by surprise.

"Where is he?" Donnall demanded, jerking me briefly to awareness.

"Not... far," I replied, breathless. Maintaining the connection to Michael required a substantial amount of power. As an acolyte, I was unused to carrying such a heavy burden. My reservoir of energy was being depleted at an alarming rate. I wasn't sure I would be able to hold on much longer.

"Once we get to the standing stones, I'll get the bonfire started. It ought to be going pretty good by the time rest of the Guard and the Sacred Order arrive."

Seamus's voice came to me, as though from a long distance. Earlier, I'd heard Donnall tell Seamus that he had alerted the Sacred Order that Michael had been located, and commanded the priests and the Guard to meet him at Mystery Hill to commence the Evaluation.

"Perfect," answered Donnall. "We'll leave my sister and the *advena* tied up a fair pace away, so there will be no chance they can interfere. You sure you're up for this, Seamus? I don't want you getting squeamish on me at the last minute."

"You're the Captain," replied Seamus matter-of-factly. "Orders are orders."

"Right, then. When we find them, you're in charge of Alena and Jonathan. I'll take care of the abomination myself."

There was an odd note of satisfaction in Donnall's voice. The hair on my scalp prickled with warning.

"I swear on the soul of my father, may Corvus forgive me. I've got a feeling I'm going to savor every moment of it."

CHAPTER TWELVE
Paper Tiger

Claudius Andrick
Blackwater Hills

Maledictus was the name given to males afflicted with the blood madness. A male suspected of suffering from the curse was imprisoned by the council and shunned by the tribe.

The blood of humans had weakened the tribe, had perverted Corvus's most sacred gift–the ability to change form. So if the blood was strong in some males, it was not strong enough. Their cells were wired to achieve a state that was no longer attainable. It drove them mad, eventually, though it was not an introverted or lethargic madness. Instead, it was murderous fury and violence growing progressively worse over time. The madness eventually burned itself out, burning with it all traces of humanity. For one thus afflicted, death was imminent.

Or so the tribe and the Sacred Order believed.

Only Claudius Andrick—the highest ranking priest of the Sacred Order, the mortal charged with the formidable task of guarding the portal to the Otherworld—knew the truth. He knew that there had once been a time when those pure of blood were leaders. When the race had been strong, the Change an awesome thing to witness.

Tapered candles burned low atop the desk in Claudius's private library. Wax collected in the crude metal holders, pooled over the rims, then dried in uneven mounds upon the scarred, worn surface. Claudius knelt before a wall of shelves, and pried three stones from the surrounding mortar. He brushed the dust from his robe, laid the loosed stones aside, and reached into the hollow beneath.

His arm disappeared into the hole, halfway to his elbow, then emerged seconds later cradling several rolled-up parchments tied with knotted strips of leather.

Claudius stood up, walked across the room, and gently laid the scrolls upon the desk. He sorted through them briefly. When he found what he sought, he looked up at the man who had come to him seeking answers. A fellow priest, this man was someone Claudius trusted implicitly. After hearing that Alena had found the ancient skulls in the tomb, Claudius knew what he needed to do.

"He is the Merula, Tarren," Claudius said.

When Tarren Campbell stared at him blankly, Claudius held an unrolled parchment out for Tarren's perusal.

"The Merula," he repeated. "It's what the ancients called those of us gifted with the ability to take the god's hallowed form."

Tarren took the page from Claudius's hand. The edges were tattered and worn by the years, the ink discolored and smudged in places. He leaned into the wavering candle light, the better to read the rows of tiny, flowing script.

When he finished, he stared, open-mouthed at Claudius. Then the light of understanding replaced the shock and confusion that had clouded Tarren's eyes. Claudius knew they had all looked thus since Michael's transformation from man to Beast. Shocked, awed—and most of all, terrified.

"Claudius," he breathed. "Do you realize what this means?"

Claudius did not reply, instead let Tarren take a moment to absorb the significance of what he'd just been shown.

"I was not in the dungeon the day Innes was killed. I did not see the Change for myself, would have said it was impossible…"

Tarren grimaced, and shook his head. "In fact, I *did* say it was impossible. Even when she brought the skull to me as proof. But, Claudius, this scroll dates back hundreds of years! How can it be that Michael Singleton's blood is so pure?"

Tarren gripped the parchment with shaking fingers. "What should we do next? How do we control him? He must harbor a great deal of resentment for us. Doubtless, he will never forgive the Sacred Order for what we have done to him."

Claudius nodded. "You understand," he said. "Michael Singleton is the Merula. None of us can stand against him."

"Do the others know?" asked Tarren. "You need not tell them, Claudius. It is enough that we let Michael live, isn't it? Maybe your daughter might somehow be able to control him. Alena could get him to submit to her author—"

"No!" interrupted Claudius. "If we admit this publicly, we risk facing our own executions. You must swear upon your immortal soul that you will guard this secret, for it is a secret known only to the

Guardian of the Dead. I am forbidden to share it with anyone. Except my successor."

Tarren's eyes widened, as comprehension dawned. "You are choosing me, Claudius? But Alena is next in line."

"My daughter is no longer suitable for the position. She has bonded with a cursed man. The priests will never stand for it."

The shaking in Tarren's fingers spread throughout his body. The parchment fluttered in his hand like the wing of an injured bird. "You're right," he breathed. "May Corvus have mercy."

Claudius stood beside him, emotions churning, restless like the river. What he'd witnessed in the dungeon the day Innes was killed played over and over in his mind, until the memory took on the blurred and disjointed quality of a nightmare.

Members of the Guard and the Sacred Order watched in horror as Michael growled and snarled and writhed upon the floor — fighting the Change, screaming and howling his fury. Claudius had been afraid that Michael might seriously damage himself in the struggle, had been ready to command Innes's men to remove the restraints.

It was doubtful the guards would have heeded the command, however. And by then, it was too late. Seconds later, out of nowhere, his daughter appeared.

Claudius remembered feeling a sense of relief that Alena had been spared the horror of the transformation. She reached for the latch, and opened the door. The Beast raced past them, up the stairs. Innes lay, ravaged, in a pool of blood on the dungeon floor. One of Claudius's oldest and dearest friends...

Gone in an instant.

If Michael Singleton were to be given absolute power, thought Claudius, *Which one of them would be next?*

Claudius would tell Tarren Campbell what he must—enough to preserve the tribe as a whole, and the Sacred Order, in particular. There were many things his successor needed to learn, and Claudius would do his best to educate him. His conscience demanded he do nothing less. For there were secrets only the Guardian of the Dead was privy to, and someone else must be aware, in case something happened to him.

Claudius took the parchment from Tarren, and rolled it up. He replaced the ties, then gathered the other scrolls and returned them to their hiding place beneath the floor.

As the last stone dropped into place—again interring secrets never meant to be uncovered—an insistent knock sounded on the Library door.

"Open up, Claudius!" shouted the Captain of the Guard. "The abomination has been found!"

* ~ * ~ *

Claudius stood apart from the Sacred Order. A few feet to his right, around the rectangular stone table used for special ceremonies, sat members of the council. He had a history with each and every one of them—with nearly everyone in the small, close-knit tribe.

Claudius, like most of them, had never been outside the protection of the miles of mountains and forest known as Blackwater Hills. He knew, through written history, that the place had been chosen by the children of Corvus for its isolation and abundance of natural resources. Humans had thus far been unwilling or unable to tame the harsh environment, opting instead to reside in places more hospitable to their delicate constitutions.

The descendants of the Beast god, however were well-equipped for such an environment, and the remote location ensured the survival of their race. None were under any illusions about successfully living amongst ordinary humans. For to live in a world where they would be forced to deny their heritage, and be unable to openly and freely honor their god, would mean the end of the priesthood— possibly the end of Corvus, Himself.

What happened to gods who were no longer worshipped? Did they meet the equivalent of human death? Perhaps, thought Claudius, the energy emitted by those who believe, is the only thing keeping the gods alive.

The children of Corvus were not forced to live in Blackwater Hills against their will. There were those who had opted to permanently reside in Ashland, and other places, altogether. Of that small number, some occasionally returned to visit friends and family. Others, such as Stella and Andrew Simon Singleton, had never been seen or heard from again. The Sacred Order did not forbid anyone leaving, unless it was believed that the individual suffered from the blood madness.

Sacred Law was unassailable—a venerated doctrine, never questioned. It been written by a group of men who called themselves the Sacred Order. They had come together, long ago, to overthrow the leader known as the Tyrannical Merula. These men, Claudius's distant predecessors, wanted to end the practice of giving one man ultimate authority over the tribe. They believed that the pure blood of Corvus had been tainted by human blood, weakened to the point that the Merula were no longer in control of their abilities.

Horrific legends of the Tyrannical Merula were legion, and were often used by parents to keep unruly children in line. It was decided that from then on, any male who showed signs of the having inherited the god's gifts would be labeled as cursed.

Thus began the practice of executing cursed males, in accordance with the ritual outlined in Sacred Law. After the uprising, leadership of the tribe was given over to the Sacred Order. Any mention of the Merula or their former roles as leaders had been stricken from the Law.

One priest, named the Guardian of the Dead, had been entrusted to keep the secret scrolls. It was through this priest, that the spells to open the portals to the Otherworld and the Shadowlands were passed down. In the days of the ancients, it had been the Merula, Himself who had kept the secret. According to the scrolls, the Merula had the ability to travel through the doors to the Otherworld and the Shadowlands, and back again. All males with the ability to transform were also capable of navigating the portal. However, not all of them succeeded in making their way back. The one who passed this test and returned, was given the title.

Claudius turned his attention to the squat stone chamber in the center of the standing stones, and wondered what was taking so long. It seemed like hours since Tarren had entered to begin the ritual.

An infusion of *aconitum napellus* had been prepared by Jackson—one of three that Michael would be made to drink during the course of the ritual. The poison would act as a sedative, subdue him, and make him easier to control. It would not kill him, for the children of Corvus had a natural immunity to the plant that was fatal if ingested by ordinary humans.

Though it was effective in controlling the more aggressive symptoms of *Maledictus,* this special brew of wolfsbane was only used in the *Ritus de Supplicium.* Much stronger than ordinary ceremonial wine, the brew was given to the cursed in order to prevent them from using their greater strength to overpower those charged with preserving the safety of the tribe.

Claudius's gaze wandered over the assemblage. He spotted Donnall Maxwell, feeding logs into the bonfire. Innes's only son was not much like his father, either in looks or temperament. Claudius was aware of the rivalry between Donnall and Alena, but had never intervened on his daughter's behalf. He had his reasons, but now was not the time to ruminate upon them. In this instance, Claudius knew, Donnall was operating well within the Law.

In an uncharacteristic act of mercy to spare them the trauma of watching the ritual, Donnall had secured Alena and the *advena,* Jonathan Lance in the forest, a fair distance from Mystery Hill. Claudius felt sorry for Alena, but he had no choice.

It was unfortunate that his daughter was being hurt by what was happening, but Michael Singleton could not be allowed to live. The very fabric of the tribe would unravel, and a future in which Michael as the Merula ruled the tribe was not a future in which Claudius wished to dwell.

Nothing good can come of it, he told himself. This was the only way. Maledictus must be put to death, according to Sacred Law. Going against the Law would signal the end of their race.

Claudius bowed his head. He felt suddenly weary of carrying the weight of what he was. He remembered telling Cora—ages ago, it seemed—that he was a priest first, before he was a father. As much as he loved his daughter, there was too much at stake. He could not afford to give in to feelings of familial love and obligation. The life they knew, the tribe as whole, could not survive it.

Alena… Please forgive me for what I am about to do.

As dusk crept through the Blackwater forest, Death hovered over the standing stones on Mystery Hill. Impatient, Death tapped his foot in annoyance, snapped his fingers, and ordered them to get on with the proceedings.

Claudius watched as they dragged Michael, bound in heavy iron, from the Oracle Chamber. He had to admit, there was a fearsome beauty to the man they shoved roughly toward the fire. He radiated vitality, as though through his veins pumped more pure, more primitive blood.

Those who had witnessed the change the day Innes was killed, would guard the secret after the ritual was over. The wolfsbane infusions had done their job well, so no one watching the execution would bear witness to the most sacred and terrifying of Corvus's gifts. Thanks to the potion, the rest of the tribe would only remember that Michael was not quite a Beast—nor yet was he a man.

Maledictus.

They dragged him toward the raging bonfire, as they beat at him with long, thick branches — thwarting every attempt he made to escape the fate that awaited him. Not that he could escape, shackled and chained as he was. He was foaming at the mouth, tearing at his bonds with raw and bleeding fingers. Blood leaked from his wounds, wound thin trails down the backs of his hands, over the rusted iron encasing his wrists.

When the macabre procession reached the edge of the firepit, they handed the prisoner over to the Captain of the Guard. Michael ceased to struggle. He lifted his head. Disheveled ink black hair spilled over savage, bloodshot eyes.

"Help us, Jonathan," he implored, his voice a husky, ravaged whisper. *"Make them stop!"*

CHAPTER THIRTEEN
The Worst That Can Happen

J. Lance Sr.
Blackwater Hills

The Blackwater forest was never silent, even at night, but Jonathan could sense an audible stillness in the air. Clouds hung above the mountains, pregnant with moisture, hazy moonlight peeking through tears in the gauzy fabric.

As Jonathan gazed through the trees, his mind replayed the events of the last few weeks. His palms were cold, and wet with sweat. His forehead throbbed from the pain of a headache.

His bound fingers itched for the notebook and pen in his backpack. He wanted to transform what was happening into fiction, so it would make sense to him. Jonathan wanted the story to have a clear beginning, middle, and end—with a poignant theme underlying at all. Then, perhaps, he could tie it all together and find some sort of deeper meaning.

The Incredible Adventures of Normal Man and Werewolf Boy captured in metaphors, anecdotes, and allegories, condensed between the pages of a book. It would then seem as though what was about to happen served some kind of greater purpose, or was part of a larger whole.

To his right—bound by ropes to a tree, just as he was—Alena moaned in her sleep. His heart skipped a beat as he glanced over. Leaves rustled, as she shifted position. He heard her mumble something, but he couldn't make it out.

"What did you say?"

He asked as a means to distract himself from the morbid contemplation of their situation, rather than out of any genuine desire to know. Alena answered anyway.

"I said, he should have used chains to tie us up, instead of rope. I might be able to get my hands loose."

More rustling of leaves, as Alena resumed sawing the thick rope that bound her wrists around the rough tree bark. She gave it up about fifteen minutes later, collapsing against the trunk with a defeated sigh.

"Jonathan?"

"What?"

"Aren't you even going to *try* to get free?"

Something in her tone, some small inflection— the implication that he might actually be able to do something to stop this madness, but preferred not to bother—pricked his temper.

"What do you suggest I do?" He sneered.

Their gazes met through a shaft of moonlight, and the fear in her eyes struck him viscerally, like a knife to the gut. Perhaps, deep down, Jonathan had convinced himself there was a chance that Michael would pass the Evaluation, and the Sacred Order would set him free. If so, the look on Alena's face told him plainly that she believed otherwise. She knew her tribe far better than he did. It would be most unwise to doubt her judgment.

Unwise, yes.

Maybe even stupid.

But he had to believe in something.

Didn't he?

Silvery light spilled through the canopy of leaves, outlining Alena's tangled mass of reddish— gold hair, the stubborn tilt of her delicately pointed chin. She turned her head, but not before Jonathan noticed the tears trailing silently over her cheeks. A chill swept through him. His arms and legs began to tremble, though his palms and underarms were drenched in sweat. He closed his eyes, and leaned his head against the tree he was tied to.

The word *surreal* didn't come close to describing the cauldron of emotions bubbling inside him. For the first time in his life, he was absolutely vulnerable, indescribably confused, and... *Dismayed* was a better word, he supposed. Though the word sounded slightly tame to his inner ear, and did not allude to the paralyzing fear that made it impossible to entertain a coherent thought long enough to form a plan that might actually work.

These circumstances were too far out of his experience for his rational mind to accept them as reality. Never had he envisioned himself caught in such a conundrum.

Sure you have, Normal Man. You've cast yourself as the hero of your own story plenty of times. You just never believed that imagination has the power to conjure reality. And everyone knows that if the great J. Lance Sr. doesn't believe in something, it can't possibly be true.

Interminable hours passed. Eventually, he succumbed to an uneasy, dream-filled sleep, but was startled awake by the raucous cry of a bird. Cold rain pelted his head like tiny pellets. The drops made sharp *ping-pin- ping* sounds when they landed on the ground, like nails being struck by a steel hammer. Jonathan tilted his face to the sky, and cracked open his parched lips, hoping some of the droplets would land on his tongue and ease the thirst that was fast becoming painful.

He managed to swallow a bit of the precious liquid, but it wasn't nearly enough. Groaning in frustration, he jerked frantically against his bonds. It was a reflex he'd developed during the past several hours. One, he was sure, that only lent credence to the theory that he'd lost his grip on reality.

After about ten minutes, he gave up fighting the ropes, and turned his head to see if Alena was awake—if she'd borne witness to his embarrassing fit of hysteria. Her eyes were closed, her full lips slightly parted, her breathing deep and even.

Jonathan studied her profile, wondering what it was about her that had caught Michael's interest. She was pretty enough, for sure, but not unusually so. As he stared, it occurred to him that Alena Andrick was the first woman he'd ever known Michael to show a serious interest in.

His nephew was an exceptionally good-looking man, but it seemed Michael's illness had held him back from getting too close to anyone. Talk about baggage. How do you explain to a potential girlfriend that you might be a werewolf?

Might be a werewolf?

Whether he liked it or not, Jonathan realized it was time to admit the truth. Not that he was really sure *what* the truth was, exactly. His journey through the Great Shield into Blackwater Hills, had made him question things he thought he'd already figured out, had burned to ashes all his long held convictions and preconceived notions about the nature of God and man.

He was now certain of nothing.

Truth. Logic. Reality.

He realized that for so long they had been his gods, his Holy Trinity. Infallible and all-powerful. But nothing lasts forever. They—just like everyone and everything he had ever put faith in—had finally betrayed him.

Truth was elusive and ethereal. He'd caught glimpses of its shadow in twilight, but like a ghost, it vanished with the light.

Logic appeared to depend on one's perspective. For instance, maybe things only made sense because he wanted them to. Maybe there was no natural order, no law of the jungle. Maybe everything really was a random series of accidents, and nothing was impossible.

Reality—his least favorite of the trinity—was too loud, too intense. He did his best to ignore it, but it demanded his attention, knew exactly how to push his buttons, and would not be satisfied until it had extracted every drop of childlike innocence from his soul. Until every burst of laughter had been paid for with a bout of sorrow.

Admittedly, it was a strange time to be having such revelations. But bound and helpless as he was, Jonathan's mind was awhirl.

It was as though he had become the conduit for answers to all the philosophical questions no one cared about. Jonathan knew the world would not mourn the loss—even if they somehow found out that he had discovered the answers, but had been unable to write them down. They were the lucky ones, he figured. For in the end, all he had really managed to do was unearth more questions.

Jonathan's muscles cramped painfully, protesting the forced inactivity, while his imagination conjured all manner of frightful creatures lurking in the mist. He tried to convince himself that the noises he heard were not the footsteps of someone—or some*thing*—coming closer, that it was only the rustle of wind through the underbrush. He tried to control his reaction to the noise, clamp down on his emotions, and turn off everything except clearheaded logic.

It was an impossible feat, a fact that frightened him more than the unseen presence that may or may not have been creeping up on them.

Alena stirred beside him. Jonathan watched her slow rise to wakefulness, noticed the way her shoulders slumped as Reality crept in to remind her where she was, ending the brief respite that sleep had offered.

For what seemed an unusually long time, she did not move or speak. Then she tossed her head, as though to clear the tangled strands of hair from her face. Her glazed eyes glittered with tiny pinpricks of light; it seemed she was looking not at him, but inward, at something he could not see.

Without the slightest warning and with no apparent cause, she arched her back, straining as far as her bonds would allow. A pain-filled cry emerged from her lips. Her body was wracked with spasms, and her chest heaved with every breath. Jonathan did the only thing he was able, and shouted her name over and over in a desperate, impotent effort to focus her attention.

Is she having a seizure? He frantically wondered. Perhaps she was an epileptic. Or maybe she suffered from diabetes and had gone too long without adequate food or water.

What the hell did he know? He wasn't a doctor. He was nothing but a fucking useless genre novelist preoccupied with fucking useless ideals. He couldn't actually do anything to save Michael or help Alena.

All he *could* do, apparently, was watch them suffer and write about it later.

The spasms ceased as abruptly as they had started. Alena sagged in her bonds, and slumped against the base of the tree. Her delicate features were contorted in a grimace of pain, a deep frown etched into the center of her forehead. Her eyes were closed, her breathing rapid and shallow.

"Are you all right?" Jonathan called out over the gulf that separated them. In reality it was only a few feet, but it may as well have been miles; captive as he was, he couldn't reach her.

She didn't answer immediately. Her eyelids slid open. She moaned softly, and her head lolled drunkenly from side to side.

"Help us, Jonathan," she pleaded, her voice hoarse and trembling, barely audible. *"Make them stop!"*

* ~ * ~ *

"So, the word advena means, 'outsider,' right?" Jonathan asked, as he took a sip from his mug of sweet mint tea. "Someone who is not a descendant of Corvus, in other words?"

Jackson nodded. "Outsider, or enemy. To us, they mean the same."

"What about humans who are not witches? Did the children of Time try to harm your beast god, too?"

Jackson reached for his mug of ceremonial wine. Out of the corner of his eye, Jonathan saw Michael pick up his own cup of wine, and raise it to his lips.

Jonathan had not been offered any wine, so he smoked one of the joints he kept inside the pocket of his jacket.

"Not exactly," Jackson answered. "But humans fear what they do not understand. The blood of the tribe has been diluted, none of us can achieve transformation, but we are still children of Corvus. Tempus is a greedy god, and so are her offspring. Humans are not capable of living peacefully alongside a race so much more powerful than themselves. They would attempt to destroy us, or enslave us, for that is their nature. We must obey the commands our Father set down in Sacred Law. Our survival as a race depends upon it."

Michael laughed, bitterly. "I will never understand how ridding the tribe of its most powerful males makes us stronger. Why would Corvus want us to destroy those of his sons who are most like Him?"

"You and I know the answer too well, Michael," Jackson chastised his nephew. *He took a sip of his wine before offering Jonathan an explanation.*

"Males who are cursed cannot control their powers. They are a danger to themselves, and others. The inability to transform drives them mad, and turns them into vicious creatures. There is no cure. They all die from the disease eventually, but considerable damage can be done in the meantime.

"Let me assure you, Jonathan, if you'd ever had the misfortune to observe a man ravaged body and soul by the blood madness, you would agree that is the only way to end their suffering."

Jonathan recalled all the conversations he'd had with Michael about the "disease" that Michael believed he suffered from. It was the reason they had made this journey from Ashland to Blackwater Hills, because Michael was convinced that the cure was hidden here, somewhere.

But if that were so, Jonathan wondered, then why wouldn't a tribe doctor—a Medicus, *such as Jackson Singleton—know anything about it?*

Jonathan glanced at Michael, a question in his eyes. Michael, preoccupied with glaring at Jackson, took no notice.

"You say we execute them out of mercy, and yet we consider those with the disease an abomination. Sacred Law forbids them entry into Corvus's domain, and their souls are condemned to wander the Shadowlands. Perhaps our Sacred Law was given to us not by Corvus, but by those who had the most to gain from adherence to its dictates."

A shadow darkened Jackson's eyes. His thin lips tightened, deepening the lines that bracketed his mouth.

"It is a sin to question the word of the god. We must have faith in Sacred Law, trust that Corvus has a greater purpose that we do not fully understand."

Michael drained his cup, and set it aside. Jackson reached for it, and poured more wine. Michael nodded his thanks, and cradled the mug in his work-roughened hands.

Jonathan sighed in frustration, unable to comprehend such blind devotion to a god.

"It's a disease, Jackson. A sickness. *You said it, yourself. Your people bemoan the fact that there is no cure, yet you isolate yourselves from modern civilization and cling to antiquated ideals and practices. I don't believe you are aware of the tremendous advances western medicine has made in the last century. Good Lord, your treatments are primitive and barbaric! Do those who suffer from heart disease or cancer get burned alive in a ceremonial bonfire?"*

Jackson stiffened. Michael raised his eyebrows, staring at Jonathan as though he'd never seen him before.

Jonathan cleared his throat, and sipped at his tea. "Well, I'm just saying..." he finished, lamely.

"Human diseases do not afflict the children of Corvus," Jackson answered after a tense silence. "Age kills most of us, and we are not immune to poison, infection, or serious injury. We are mortal, Jonathan, but aside from the blood madness, our people are free of the sicknesses that afflict humans."

Jonathan's head spun as he thought of his wife, Stella. She had never once been sick in the nine years they had been married. Neither had Michael, or Andrew Simon. It had never occurred to Jonathan to wonder why before, but now Jackson's words triggered memories of how puzzled and impatient Stella had acted whenever he had gotten sick.

Jonathan stared at Michael. Michael met his gaze and shrugged, as though in apology.

Sorry, Jay, *his look implied.* I would have told you, but you never asked.

Indeed.

Jonathan opened his mouth, intending to voice one of the myriad logical explanations that were clamoring in his brain like unruly toddlers. The problem was, none could indisputably refute Jackson beliefs beyond a shadow of a doubt. There was always a chance – slim, though it may have been – that maybe it actually was true, and Jonathan was the one clinging to antiquated ideals and practices.

Such as logical reasoning and scientific principles.

As Jonathan sat with his mouth half open, waiting for something coherent to emerge, the door to Jackson's cabin burst open, and a tall, hooded figure filled the doorway. A hand emerged from beneath the cloak, and peeled back the red cotton hood, revealing a shaggy mane of light brown hair and the masculine beauty of a fallen angel.

When the young man shook the hair out his eyes, the effect of physical perfection was somewhat diminished by a thick scar that bisected his left eyebrow. Bright green eyes—hard and cold, seemingly devoid of conscience or empathy—scrutinized the three men gathered round the table.

"Greetings, Donnall," Jackson welcomed the intruder.

The newcomer scowled, and waved an impatient hand in Michael's direction.

"I've only come to deliver an invitation," he said, sounding as though it was a task he resented performing. "Innes and Cora would like to invite the three of you to eat at the Maxwell's table during the feast this afternoon."

Michael raised his mug in salute. "I guess some things have changed around here. Should I be concerned, Donnall? Or have they made you promise to behave yourself during the celebration?" It wasn't like Michael to pick a fight. Something was different about his nephew, but Jonathan couldn't put his finger on it.

"What's that you're drinking?" he asked, trying to sound casual.

Michael cocked his head to the side, and appraised Jonathan through half—closed eyelids.

"Ceremonial wine. Made from elderberries and wolfsbane. A little bitter, but after the first couple swallows, your mouth goes numb and you don't even taste it."

Jonathan's eyebrows shot straight to his hairline. "Wolfsbane? Good Lord, that's poison, Michael!"

Michael gazed thoughtfully down into his cup. "Not for us."

Donnall rolled his eyes, and stalked into the kitchen. As he bent to open one of the cupboards, the fabric of his cloak stretched tightly across his broad shoulders. He grabbed a jug from inside, uncorked the top, and lifted it to his lips. An Adam's Apple bobbed up and down, as he drank deeply. The jug descended slowly, and he leaned one hip against the kitchen counter.

Jonathan could feel the young man's gaze on him, like two emerald glaciers. It was as though Donnall had already decided they were enemies, and was sizing him up for the inevitable confrontation. Jonathan tried to suppress the involuntary shudder that stare invoked, and excused himself to use the outhouse. When he returned, Donnall was gone, and Jackson was bent over the table refilling Michael's mug of wine.

"We'd better get going," Jackson said. "The feast begins in a few hours."

Michael drained his mug in one draught. "I guess I'm as ready as I'm gonna get," he said, swaying a bit as he wiped his mouth with the sleeve of his shirt.

Jackson led the way outside. On the way to the castle, Jonathan lagged behind, wishing he could see through the wall of Michael's wavy black hair, and figure out what was going on inside his head. Jonathan had never seen his nephew drunk before. Michael claimed that alcohol had no effect on the children of Corvus. Jonathan was willing to suspend his disbelief enough to accept that Michael's genetic makeup might be somewhat different than his own, but…

Wolfsbane was a poison.
Fatal, if ingested.

* ~ * ~ *

"What do you want me to do?" Jonathan shouted.

His heart was pounding in a disconnected rhythm. He clenched his jaw to stop his teeth from chattering. Fear churned in his gut like a nest of poisonous vipers, eating him alive from the inside out.

"I can't get loose! What the hell is going on?"

"It burns," she rasped, her face and limbs contorted with pain. Her eyelids flickered, and she appeared to be losing consciousness.

Jonathan didn't know how, but he was certain that *somehow* Alena knew that the Sacred Order were actually—maybe even right at that very moment—going through with the plan to execute Michael.

By now, there was no doubt in his mind that Michael had killed Donnall's father, but he couldn't seem to make himself care about that. Whether or not the vengeance was justified, made no difference to the way he felt. If Michael ended up dead...

Like Stella...

He shouted Alena's name, but there was no response. With a primal roar, he twisted and writhed against the ropes that restrained him like a wild animal caught in a trap. Logic and reason cowered in the corner, hands clapped firmly over their eyes, for they did not want to see how quickly he'd been reduced to the primitive creature that the veneer of civilization had never quite been able to mask.

Adrenaline surged through his limbs, and the rope securing his wrists around the tree trunk snapped under the pressure.

A loud sob escaped his throat—a mixture of surprise, triumph and profound relief. Jonathan pushed away from the tree, and crawled on hands and knees to the spot where Alena was tied. After checking to make sure she was still breathing, he went behind the tree to untie her.

His numb fingers fumbled with the complicated knots, and he swore loudly and vehemently as the rough hemp shredded his fingernails. Misty drizzle changed to heavy rain, and by the time he managed to free Alena's wrists, they were both thoroughly soaked.

He carried her away from the tree, laid her down upon a pile of wet leaves, and checked her pulse. Her heart seemed to be beating a little too fast, but Jonathan had no idea what a normal pulse was. She moaned softly, mumbling words he strained to hear. The patter of raindrops, and the sound of his own heartbeat thundering in his ears, drowned out everything else. He knelt down, grabbed her shoulders in both hands, and leaned in, close to her face.

"Alena, wake up. We have to get out of here!"

Even as he shouted the words, he realized how ridiculous they were.

Get out of here how? Where the fuck was here?

He shook her, none-too-gently. Her lips parted on a harsh expulsion of breath, and her head lolled drunkenly.

"Goddammit!" He exclaimed in frustration. He released her and stood up, pacing back and forth beside her unconscious body—hands on hips, his thoughts swarming in his head like a pack of angry bees—and tried to figure out what to do next.

Jonathan's first impulse was to pick up Alena and start walking. Direction didn't matter. All that mattered was getting far away before Donnall or Seamus returned. He did not doubt they would come back after they finished with Michael, and he didn't want to be anywhere near this spot when they did. But what about Michael? Jonathan couldn't just leave him at the mercy of those savages and their barbaric concept of justice. But how could he ever hope to find him, lost in this vast and overgrown wilderness?

Wind gusted through the leaves. Cold rain stung his head and face like sharp needles. Jonathan stopped pacing, took a shuddering breath, and looked around. A majestic ring of rugged mountains surrounded endless miles of primeval forest. Nothing but trees and sky, rivers and streams, with no roads or buildings to serve as landmarks and break up the monotony.

You're never going to make it out of here alive, Normal Man.

"Shut up," Jonathan hissed out loud at the annoying voice in his head. He said a silent prayer of thanks, when the voice appeared to listen.

He didn't want to give in to panic and despair, didn't want to give up, but didn't know what else to do. He knew he wasn't thinking clearly, and didn't trust himself to make the right decision.

Jonathan rushed back to Alena's side, and shook her again. When she didn't respond, he slipped his arms beneath her body, lifting a bit to test her weight.

She was small and fine-boned, couldn't have weighed more than a hundred pounds soaking wet, but... Well, a hundred pounds was a hundred pounds, and he hadn't eaten or had anything to drink in over twelve hours.

Jonathan remembered how Michael had carried Alena through miles of tangled forest without breaking a sweat, and felt an incongruous stab of jealousy. Then—to chase away the guilt and soothe his wounded pride—he reminded himself that Michael was nearly half his age.

Not to mention the fact that Michael was also a werewolf, and it was common knowledge that werewolves were stronger than ordinary humans.

Jonathan figured that the odds of finding the old dirt road and the car he'd left parked there were dismal, but he had to try. There were, after all, no other options.

Clutching Alena to his chest, he stood up carefully, staggering a bit before recovering his balance. Grunting with effort, he shifted her weight so her head rested atop his shoulder.

He titled his head and squinted up at the sky. The sun was barely visible through a sheet of thick gray clouds. Jonathan headed west—or, what he thought was west—in the opposite direction of the dawn.

That's when he noticed the smoke, travelling upwards, through the wall of trees. Drumbeats pounded a primitive rhythm. As he got closer, he heard the shouts, the desperate cries.

And he knew.

He *knew*.

They were too late.

CHAPTER FOURTEEN
Doors

Justin
The Otherworld

"I couldn't save him, Mack. We lost another one to the Witch, and Raven doesn't even seem to care."

"You got balls, Justin. I'll give you that. Asking Raven to open the portal could have been the final straw to get you demoted for good. He must have a soft spot for you, or somethin'."

Justin paced like a tiger in a too—small cage. He wanted badly to punch something, and struggled to keep himself under control.

"There has to be something I can do. Some way into the Shadowlands."

Mack looked at him, horrified. "You can't do that! There might be a way in, but there ain't no way out. You'd be lost in there with him, and what good would that do?"

Justin stopped pacing, and ran his fingers through his hair in frustration.

"I know it, Mack. I just wanted to save this one so bad. I can't even explain it."

He took a deep breath, and turned away from the wall. He didn't want to watch anymore. It was too painful.

"Mind if I take a break till the end of our shift?" he asked his companion.

"Sure," Mack said, good—naturedly. "Take as much time as you need."

Justin turned to leave, but not before he noticed the look of pity in Mack's eyes. He supposed Mack understood as well as anyone, what he was feeling. It happened to all of them, at least once.

"Thanks, man. I owe you one."

* ~ * ~ *

J. Lance Sr.
Ashland, Maine

"Explain this disease, Michael. What are the symptoms? How does it feel?"
"It feels like I'm losing my fucking mind. You want all the sordid details? You writing a book on it, or something?"

"Maybe." Jonathan grinned, sheepishly. "I must admit, I find the subject fascinating."

Michael scowled. "I thought alcohol would numb me, but no matter how much I drank, I couldn't find the Balance."

"I've never seen you drunk, Michael."

"Cause it didn't work. I just said that, didn't I?"

"How much did you drink?"

"Two bottles of whiskey, and three bottles of wine – which were terrible, by the way. Not like the wine the tribe makes, that's for sure."

Jonathan's horrified gaze flew to the liquor cabinet. "Not my good French wine?" "Nasty stuff, Jay. You should thank me for sparing you."

Jonathan's jaw dropped. "Please tell me you're joking. I've been saving those bottles since my wedding day. Stella and I planned to drink them next year, on our tenth anniversary."

"Then Aunt Stella ought to thank me, too."

Jonathan sighed. "They were a gift from my cousin, Robert. Cheap bastard. I should have known."

"I'll replace them," Michael offered.

"What do you know about wine?"

"Apparently, more than you do."

Jonathan reached for his coffee, took a small sip, then stared down into the swirling, dark liquid. "Can we talk honestly, Michael?"

"Don't we always?"

Jonathan shrugged. "Yes, but I'm worried about you. I understand that I'm not your father, but sometimes I get the feeling you don't completely trust me."

Michael stared out the large bay window in silence. Jonathan studied his nephew's handsome profile, looking for cracks in the armor. He realized it had been a very long time since he had seen Michael smile.

"You know me better than anyone, Jay," he answered, after a time. "I trust you more than I've ever trusted anyone – even Aunt Stella and Andrew

Simon. But trust only takes me so far, and then I can't go any further. I'm sorry."

"Good Lord, don't apologize! I didn't say it to make you feel bad."

"I know, Jay." Michael's voice was like sandpaper, rough and rasping. A muscle jumped in his cheek, and his hands curled into fists, sliding back and forth over the soft leather arms of the chair he was sprawled in.

Jonathan felt the silence, like a heavy weight pressing down on him. His heart fluttered anxiously, for no particular reason. He cleared his throat, grabbed a dog—eared stack of typewritten pages, and perused them with half—hearted interest.

"It's boring," he muttered, to change the subject. "Utterly lifeless, and pathetically self—conscious. I should just scrap the whole thing, and start over."

Michael glanced over. "How much have you written?"

"About eighty pages. I keep telling myself to work on something else, but the thought of starting a new project makes me nauseous."

Jonathan grimaced, and cast the pages aside. "I think I'll go for a walk in the garden. Perhaps my muse is hiding among the lilies and hostas, waiting for me to come and find her. You can join me, if you'd like."

Michael shook his head. "I have to leave soon, for work. Is Aunt Stella's plane coming in tomorrow?"

"Monday. The day after tomorrow. She wanted to stay an extra day to tour Caerlaverock Castle in Scotland. Though after six weeks of touring every castle in the United Kingdom, I can't imagine how

she could stand to see another one," he teased, *affectionately. "Andrew Simon has decided to stay in London for a while."*

"What for?"

"He's met someone. They're planning to set up house – or, whatever it is that Andrew does."

"A woman?" Michael asked.

Jonathan shook his head.

Michael rose from his seat with a graceful fluidity uncommon in a man of his size.

"I'll let you get back to your work. See you later, Jay," Michael called out as he exited the study.

Jonathan stared at his nephew's retreating back.

Something's wrong. *He thought.* Michael's hiding something.

But, for the life of him, he couldn't figure out what.

* ~ * ~ *

Michael Singleton
The Shadowlands

Alena's mind had yielded no secrets. He'd been unable to locate the door to the Otherworld—let alone figure out how to open it. As for Corvus, the Beast god seemed to have turned His back on His sons altogether, as though to punish them for sins they didn't know they had committed.

But none of those things mattered anymore. Despite his earlier denials, deep down, Michael knew that he—not *Bestiae*—was guilty of Innes's murder. Just as he knew, innately, that the Sacred Order had the right of it. He was an abomination, unfit to live. A danger to every man, woman, and child he came into contact with.

Even Alena.

His *lifemate.*

The woman who might, even now, be nourishing his cursed seed within her womb.

Michael hoped that if Alena was pregnant with his child, that the child would be a girl. Like her, with honest eyes, creamy white skin, and long silky auburn hair.

Michael stared into the cold green eyes of the man to whom he owed this spiritual debt. The bitter taste of wolfsbane coated the back of his tongue, and a calm feeling of acceptance flooded through him. All the fight drained out of his body. Donnall's lips curved upwards in a satisfied smile. Michael closed his eyes and accepted his fate.

And then he found himself...

Here.

Alone, on Mystery Hill.

Michael did not remember being burned alive. Although he knew it had happened, the details—fear, despair, betrayal, pain—were lost to him. Though the memory seemed insubstantial, he could recall his final hours. When he did so, he felt a grudging admiration for the machinations of the god of fate. A clever manipulator, Fatum always found a way to restore the Balance—despite the interference of His siblings' children.

He looked around. But for himself and the humming Standing Stones, the site was deserted. It made sense, that this place would be the door between the worlds. The question was, which world was this?

The world Michael found himself in was cast in deep purple-blue twilight, a full moon shining overhead. Shadows darted about like wisps of dark smoke, lacking form or substance. He started walking toward the forest, drawn to its promise of familiar shelter.

His movements felt slow and ponderous. It seemed to be taking an eternity for his body to respond to his brain's commands. As he neared the tree line, he noticed a figure hiding behind a tree trunk. Her long dark hair was disheveled, her posture cowering and fearful.

He recognized her immediately—though the madwoman standing before him bore little resemblance to the vibrant, beautiful woman he remembered.

"Stella," he whispered, reaching out his hand. "It's me. Michael."

Tendrils of mist curled upwards from the forest floor. The woman who was once his Aunt Stella, shook her head violently.

"No tricks!" she hissed at him. "I can tell when it's a trick!"

She trembled like a rabbit being hunted by a hawk. The slightest wrong move could send her scurrying away, to be swallowed in the mist. It was his fault she was here, he realized. In May of last year, Stella Singleton Lance had died in a plane crash on her way home from Scotland. And he hadn't made sure she'd received a proper burial.

During the Ritual of Silence, The Guardian of the Dead opens the door to the Otherworld, so the souls of the children of Corvus can enter. The door stays open for three days. After three days, if the soul has not passed through the door, they are denied entrance for eternity. If the door is not opened—or the soul is unable to pass through it—the dead remain trapped in the Shadowlands.

The domain of the Witch.

"It's only me," he repeated, moving slowly, so as not to frighten her.

"Prove it," she spat, her ragged fingernails digging into the rough tree bark.

"How?" he asked, his heart breaking as he saw what her time in this world had cost her.

"Show me your beast—form," she demanded. "It's the only form the *daemons* cannot replicate."

EPILOGUE
In Vindicare

J. Lance Sr.
Blackwater Hills

Jonathan couldn't feel his feet hitting the ground, but was sure they must have been, for the hollow sound of footsteps — like a somber proclamation — echoed through the forest:

Dead—dead—dead—dead

I don't believe it, he thought. *Michael is* not *dead.*

But I saw...

Don't think about that, he told himself. If he didn't think about it, he wouldn't feel the pain. A moment would pass without the horror replaying in his mind.

Dead—dead—dead—dead

He spotted the bumper of his car sticking out of a clump of thorny weeds. The waning sun sparkled off the metal. His footsteps pounded harder, faster on the rugged forest floor.

DA—dead—DA—dead—DA—dead—DA—dead
NOTdeadNOTdeadNOTdeadNOTdead

He reach the car just as his legs gave out from under him. His fingernails tore as he scrambled frantically for the door handle. The world tilted dangerously.

Jonathan collapsed against the driver's side window, air wheezing in and out of his lungs.

What the hell was he supposed to do now? How could he go back to his life in Ashland—a normal life that now seemed so unreal and insubstantial, like an incoherent dream? None of it made sense anymore. He couldn't remember a time when he did not feel devastated, and couldn't foresee a time in which he would not feel that way.

Jonathan was destined to carry, for the remainder of his days, the gruesome memory of his nephew's body as it was consumed by flames. The screams. The crackle and roar of the massive bonfire. The smell that still lingered in the air and clung to his skin, poisoning every breath.

That horrifying image would never be erased, never lose clarity, never be something he wouldn't see every fucking waking moment of every fucking day for the rest of his fucking life.

This is all your fault, Normal Man. You should have been able to protect him. You should have listened to Andrew Simon when he warned you not to let Michael go back to Blackwater Hills. Why didn't you listen?

I'm sorry, Stella.

So fucking sorry.

* ~ * ~ *

Ashland, Maine

With trembling fingers, Jonathan closed the notebook, and unfolded the letter.

Greetings Jonathan,
I hope this letter finds you in good health.
As I read the journal you left me on that fateful day when we parted ways, I was disappointed to discover that you left out some of the most important parts of the story. However, upon further contemplation, I realized that you simply didn't have time to write it all down.
I, on the other hand, have had nothing but time these past months. Time to mourn, to remember what has happened, and wonder how I could have done things differently.
Donnall and Seamus have been clever and convincing in their lies, but I console myself with the knowledge that as long as you are alive—even so far away, in the land of the advena—*I am not alone. I can't quite accept that I will never see Michael again. It is like a wound in my soul that can never be mended. I believe that my spirit will never be at peace, but I thought that writing some of it down might ease the pain of not having my* lifemate *here in the physical world.*
After long months spent doing little but transcribing our tale, I came to realize that it won't be complete somehow, until someone else reads it. You have lost a lifemate *yourself, so I know that you can relate to the pain, the devastating sense of loss.*
The tribe believes the myth, the lie of Sacred Law which shifts the Balance too much in favor of the

Sacred Order and oppresses the ones who are more powerful. Those who can achieve the transformation threaten the absolute authority the priests have over the tribe. We condemn the Princes of our race, and claim they are unfit to live—when in reality, they should rank above even the highest ranking Guardian, for their gifts are more pure. They are the true sons of Corvus, and ought to be revered, not reviled.

I learned this shocking truth when I searched my father's library. From the dusty depths of the library, beneath loose stones in the floor, I unearthed scrolls that told of a time in our history when those who could transform were looked upon as gods-come-to-earth. By doing so, I breached the sanctity of my father's sacred chamber.

To punish this transgression, the Sacred Order voted to abort my training—giving the excuse that mating with Michael had tainted me somehow. Because of this taint, they said, they could never trust me again. There was, therefore, no chance that I would ever be initiated as a Guardian. No way would they allow me to inherit the title of Guardian of the Dead.

The following day, they began my trial for the murder of Ian MacDonald. The scrolls were returned to my father. I assume he hid them well. No one outside of the Sacred Order was aware they existed, of course, and would not have been permitted to read them anyway. Not even acolytes were allowed to read the scrolls of Sacred Law. One had to be initiated into the priesthood first—another tenet I had broken.

I am now serving out my sentence: twenty-five years confinement in the castle tower. I am allowed *visitors, and have been informed by Jackson Singleton that most of the tribe considers it a lenient punishment, in light of the severity of my sins.*

As I await the imminent birth of my child, I wonder if it is fair to bring into this harsh environment—a child who will never know his father, who will grow up hearing nothing but lies and rumors.

Judging from the massive size of my belly, instinct tells me this baby is a boy. I am going to name him Samuel, because any child born with so many strikes against him ought to at least have the ear of a god. I say a prayer every night, asking Corvus to spare my son the disease peculiar to our people. I pray that he will grow to manhood happy, healthy, and strong—untainted by the reputation of his father. Although I suppose it is up to me to make sure this happens, more often than not I feel inadequate to the task.

Should I tell our child what really happened to his father? Should I tell him the truth, that Michael was a Merula, not an abomination? Or would it be better for our son to grow up believing the lie of Sacred Law?

The hidden scrolls proclaim that once a Prince achieves the highest level of His gifts—which is known as the postmortem evolution of Bestiae *to Merula—Corvus appoints the Blackbird to serve in his army.*

The Blackbirds are soldiers in his war against his sister, the Witch—His eyes and ears to the needs and prayers of His children. So, how will I teach Michael's son to obey Sacred Law and respect the priests, when I understand how terribly they've upset the Balance?

Surely, Corvus will claim His vengeance on the Guardians for warping His sacred word with such a clever pack of lies! If I am lucky enough to still be alive when that day comes, then perhaps I might finally feel whole again.

Soon enough, I will have someone to take care of, someone to love again. My mother, Cora Maxwell, has been lecturing me ad nauseam *on what to expect once the baby is born. She makes motherhood sound like nothing but a series of unpleasant, repetitive chores, but I think it will be different for me. After all, it's not as though I'll have anything else to occupy my time.*

Until I make my journey to the Otherworld, I will think of Michael every day, will feel his loss as though part of my own soul has gone missing. I want our child to know who his father really was. I want him to know that he was conceived in love, and that the love has not died—even though a part of me can't seem to forgive Michael for leaving me.

Which brings me to the topic of your journal. Before you escaped through the Shield, you gave it to me and said that you could never again bring yourself to read it. You must now be wondering why I've asked Jackson to deliver it back to you.

All I ask, Jonathan, is for you to read the parts that I have written—Michael's story, and mine. Maybe then, you can let go of the past and begin to heal. Maybe then, I can finally do so too.

After having spent the past months of my confinement transcribing our tale, this is what I have come to understand about Michael:

If you are a wild soul, you yearn for peace. What is death, after all, but a door to another world? Reality is simply a degree of darkness, a shadow in sunlight, that moment of clarity when you know—just for a second—what it is that you see. Compared to those brief, rare moments, the rest of life is little more than an imperfect reflection of the Brighter Star.

But if you think you will become whole after death, and the primitive, animal instincts will cease forever, you are driven to search for that door—not quite sure you want to cross the threshold, but desperate to stand on the edge of it, leaning over, hoping not to fall.

Till We Meet Again,
Alena Andrick

THE END

FAMILIES OF THE TRIBE OF CORVUS:

MAXWELL
Innes Maxwell – *m.* – Cora Maxwell
                    c.
Donnall Maxwell – *m.* – Shaina MacDonald
                    c.
Alexander – *s.* – Sebastian – *s.* – Devin – *s.* – Acadia – *s.* – Jarren

Cora Maxwell – *m.* – Claudius Andrick
                c.
            Alena Andrick

SINGLETON
Branden – *s.* – Stella – *s.* – Andrew Simon – *s.* – Jared – *s.* – Jackson

Branden Singleton – *m.* – Erin Campbell
        c.
Michael Singleton – *m.* – Alena Andrick
                    c.
            Samuel Singleton

LANCE
Jonathan Lance Sr. – *m.* – Stella Singleton
                c.
        Jonathan Jr. - *s.* – Sarina

(m.- Mated *c.-* Child / Children *s.-* Siblings)

249

FAMILIES OF THE TRIBE OF CORVUS:

SINGLETON
Branden Singleton
Mated to Erin Campbell. Had one child: Michael Singleton

Stella Singleton
Mated to Jonathan Lance. Had twins: Sarina Lance and Jonathan Lance Jr.

Andrew Simon Singleton

Jared Singleton

Jackson Singleton

MAXWELL
Innes Maxwell
Mated to Cora James. Had one child: Donnall Maxwell

Donnall Maxwell
Mated to Shaina MacDonald. Had five children: Alexander Maxwell, Sebastian Maxwell, Devin Maxwell, Acadia (Cadie) Maxwell, and Jarren Maxwell

Malcolm Maxwell
Brother to Innes

ANDRICK

Anna Andrick

Allistair Andrick

Claudius Andrick
Had one child with Cora James Maxwell: Alena
Andrick mated to Michael Singleton

MAC DONALD
Seamus MacDonald

Ian MacDonald
Mated to Diana James. Had one son: Ian MacDonald,
Jr.

Shaina MacDonald
Mated to Donnall Maxwell

Kira MacDonald

KENDRICK
Medicus Simon Kendrick

Sayla Kendrick
Mother of Elise Kendrick

Elise Kendrick
Mated to Tarren Campbell

JAMES
Ivan James

Cora James
Mated to Innes Maxwell

CAMPBELL
Tarren Campbell
Mated to Elise Kendrick. Had one son: Corin
Campbell

Thomas Campbell

ALEXANDER
Corin Alexander

Nela Alexander

GLOSSARY

Advena - Outsider / Stranger

Animus Rimor – Exploring the mind

Avia - Grandmother

Cessio - Surrender

Captare – A form of hypnosis

Si placet - Please

Vernus – Spring Solstice Celebration / Birthday of Tempus

Brumalis - Winter Solstice Celebration / Birthday of Corvus

Bestiae, subimus! – Beast, submit!

Medicus – Doctor

Gratiae - Thank You

Parvi refert – It matters little / Don't worry about it

Maledictus – Cursed

Merula – Blackbird / Raven

Morbus Desicco – Draining Sickness

Ritus de Supplicium – Ritual of Execution

Stultissimi - Idiots

Vappa ac nebulo – Worthless scoundrel

Tempero – Control yourself

Meus filia – My daughter

Meus filius – My son

In Vindicare – The Claim